Nothing Like An Ocean

Kentucky Voices

Nothing Like
An Ocean

Stories

Jim Tomlinson

THE UNIVERSITY PRESS OF KENTUCKY

Several stories in this collection were previously published, some in slightly different form. "Nothing Like An Ocean" appeared in *Shenandoah* 57, no. 1 (Spring 2007). "Birds of Providence" was serialized in *Velocity Weekly*, November 1–29, 2006. A modified version of "Berliner" appeared in *Oasis Journal 2005* (Imago Press). "Rose" appeared in *Opium Magazine*, no. 6 (Spring 2008). "A Male Influence in the House" appeared in *Sou'wester* 37, no. 1 (Fall 2008).

The University Press of Kentucky

Scholarly publisher for the Commonwealth, serving Bellarmine University, Berea College, Centre College of Kentucky, Eastern Kentucky University, The Filson Historical Society, Georgetown College, Kentucky Historical Society, Kentucky State University, Morehead State University, Murray State University, Northern Kentucky University, Transylvania University, University of Kentucky, University of Louisville, and Western Kentucky University.

Editorial and Sales Offices: The University Press of Kentucky
663 South Limestone Street, Lexington, Kentucky 40508–4008
www.kentuckypress.com

13 12 11 10 09   5 4 3 2 1

Library of Congress Cataloging-in-Publication Data

Tomlinson, Jim, 1941–
  Nothing like an ocean : stories / Jim Tomlinson.
      p.   cm. — (Kentucky voices)
  ISBN 978-0-8131-2540-4 (hardcover : alk. paper)
  1. City and town life—Kentucky—Fiction. 2. Kentucky—Fiction.
I. Title.
  PS3620.O575N67 2009
  813'.6—dc22

                                    2008049851

This book is printed on acid-free paper meeting the requirements of the American National Standard for Permanence in Paper for Printed Library Materials.

Manufactured in the United States of America.

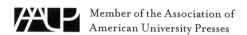

Member of the Association of
American University Presses

For Bernie and Betty

Storms approached, sent the ocean
rolling like a procession of ridges,
on and on until I believed I stood
on the mountain where my kin slept,
the wrinkled ridge and valley blue,
purpled, and frothy with dogwood.

   —Jane Hicks, "Paradise Regained"

Contents

Acknowledgments

I want to express my heartfelt appreciation to Gin Petty for her amazing patience and encouragement during the writing of these stories. Thanks to Gail Hochman, to valued readers Nancy Zafris, Cheryl Strayed, Richard Taylor, Barbara A. Fischer, Steve Lyon, and Mary Akers, and to all the wonderfully giving writers at Zoetrope Virtual Studios.

Sincere thanks to the National Endowment for the Arts and the Kentucky Arts Council for their ongoing financial support. Thanks, too, to the donors, supporters, and staff at the Carnegie Center for Literacy and Learning in Lexington, Kentucky, and the Appalachian Writers Workshop at Hindman Settlement School, places that nourish so many writers' souls.

And for their generous spirits and sage advice, a special thanks to the incredibly supportive folks at the Sewanee Writers' Conference —Wyatt Prunty and Cheri Peters, Richard Bausch, Jill McCorkle, Tony Earley, John Casey, Claire Messud, the full faculty, staff, fellows, scholars, and contributors all.

Nothing Like An Ocean

When two tickets to the over-forty singles mixer at Spivey Independent Christian Church arrived in the mail, Alton Wood thought they were a mistake. Still he couldn't help wondering. He found the discarded envelope and examined it. It was hand addressed, his name and street in slanted turquoise script, the letters neat and wide-looped. None of his high school science students used ink like that, none he had now, none he remembered from recent years. And none wrote so legibly. Perforations along one end revealed where stubs had been removed from each ticket.

"There's no return address," he told his sister Fran when she phoned that evening to ask if he needed laundry done. "The postmark is local, the stamp a World War II airplane. It's flying upside down."

"I hope you saved it," Fran said. "Misprint stamps are valuable."

"It's a normal stamp," he said, "just stuck on upside down. Whoever sent it was careless." His voice caught on the last word, a stupid choice on his part. Ill-considered. Still, not really a choice, just a word after all. For Fran, though, now silent on the line, what a wounding word it must be.

"Save it for me anyway," his sister said finally. He imagined her fidgeting hands, the pained look in her eyes.

"So it wasn't you?" he said. He stretched the coiled phone cord, wiggled it into a damped sine wave. "You didn't send the tickets?"

"You should go. Meet someone. It's time," Fran said. "But no, it wasn't me sent you those tickets."

He hadn't thought she had, not really. For one thing, Wood didn't attend church, hadn't for years, not that one or any other. And technically, he wasn't a single. This she also well knew. And to top it off, he was only thirty-eight. She was the one who'd recently turned forty. Under the loosest of interpretations, he wouldn't qualify for an over-forty mixer for another two years. Not for three years, if one gave "over-forty" its strictest interpretation.

Of course, local Independent Christians weren't known for strict interpretations. In fact, they could be quite flexible in their beliefs, dangerously unstructured, wishy-washy in a way Wood had come to believe religions should never be. Maybe some people liked their religion that way. Not Wood. He preferred commandments to vague guidelines any day.

People baffled Alton Wood. He took great pride in mastering the basics of complex processes in nature, of subatomic phenomena and interstellar dark matter, of the relativistic implications of post-Newtonian time-space. But the seeming randomness of human behavior perplexed him. Lori, for example, the inscrutable woman who was his wife until one day she decided not to be that anymore. After what they'd weathered together, the pain of losing Logan, the son they'd both loved, after surviving that, when the worst was past, *then* the woman decides to leave. Truly baffling.

Until that day, he'd thought Lori was steady. How often he'd said it—"Lori, she's the steady one." Yet there she stood, teary in the doorway, suitcase in hand, a volatile being, turning away and careening away from him. The last he'd heard, she was waitressing in Charlottesville, living there with the auto mechanic who'd rebuilt the transmission on her Volvo. Wood often imagined her with him, this slender man with greasy cuffs, the smell of gasoline on his lanky hands, a ropy man with hair poking over his T-shirt neck, a dozen rusty lug nuts weighting his pants pockets, rattling as he walked. It would be a year next month since Lori boarded a Greyhound bus with that man. Kimbro. That was his name. Some days Wood wondered if she'd ever come to her senses, if she'd ever board that bus again and come back.

"Maybe Teresa Click sent those tickets," Fran said.

"They're probably just someone's stupid mistake," he said, ready now to hang up, to forget everything those damn tickets had dredged up.

But Wood didn't tear them up, and he didn't throw them away. Instead, he lay awake that night wondering who sent them. The next morning, when he saw Fran's overloaded Buick angle-parked in front of Fat Momma's Dairy Deluxe, he parked nearby and waited. She came out carrying a Star Wars IV commemorative Super Quencher cup of Coke, a small pastry sack, and a copy of the *Louisville Courier-Journal*. He hurried across the street.

"Go with me," he said, "to that mixer thing?"

She slid into the front seat and added the newspaper to a pile on the passenger seat. The pile, tall as her shoulders, tilted against the passenger door like a drunk. In the back seat, more mounds of magazines and newspapers, burger and coffee Styrofoam, a plastic bin overflowing with saved junk mail. A tall stack of nested Quencher cups lay across everything. Thumb-sized plastic gnomes with neon hair, bright blue Smurfs, and farm and jungle animals were scattered about the car. A faded plastic cowboy straddled the rearview mirror support, riding it like a bronco. Cardboard pine trees dangled below, drab red and green, their scents spent long ago.

Fran had always been a collector, a gatherer of things. She'd had limits though. Since the whole sad business with Logan, the quirk had morphed into a kind of manic hoarding. Even Wood acknowledged that now. Still, this was not something he could broach with his sister. Not yet.

"You want me to go?" She opened the sack, took out a jelly doughnut for herself, and extended the gaping sack toward him.

"Friday night," he said, refusing with a gesture. "I'm curious. Aren't you?"

"Just curious, Alton?" She stowed the sack beside her seat.

Okay, maybe Lori *was* gone for good. He'd concede that it was possible. Maybe this was how his life would be, how his future would be, whatever he could make of it. "You're not curious?" he asked Fran again.

She shrugged and turned the key. "You drive," Fran said. She lifted off of her wood-bead seat cover and twisted her thick torso. Peering over piles, she backed out.

As she parked behind Click's Hallmark Store, it occurred to Fran that she was curious about who'd sent her brother tickets, and that curiosity made her feel uneasy. Nervous. She could bear her life, the one she lived now, if she crusted her days in certainty, confined herself to trivial matters, to acts of little consequence. Curiosity felt like a frivolous, yet vaguely dangerous, thing.

Fran hadn't always been this way. She'd been playful as a child, even wild at times, frighteningly so, thinking back now. She'd broken an arm and dislocated a shoulder falling from the garage roof. Just that, thankfully not her skull. A pale scar still snaked from the hollow of her throat to the middle of her chest, the vestige of a furrow dug by a spear point young Franny had whittled on a catalpa sprout. In high school, she'd often hitchhiked to Somerset, dancing there, sometimes hitchhiking home again. She'd slide into strangers' cars armed only with her faith and a ready smile. She shuddered now, remembering.

The Hallmark store manager, a redheaded widow named Teresa Click, was busy up front with a customer. Fran helped Teresa during busy times, selling scented candles, luminaries, angel figurines, and bright holiday ornaments behind the smaller counter. It was the kind of work Fran had sought—reasonable hours, little chance of screwing up, minimal consequences if she did.

"Teresa," Fran called when the customer left. "You didn't send my brother tickets to the over-forty mixer, did you?"

Teresa stopped straightening cards, and a puzzled expression settled on her face. "Do I know your brother?"

"Alton Wood."

"That's right," Teresa Click said. She snapped her fingers and made a check mark in the air. "That's who you are."

A damp chill ran through Fran. She drew a deep breath, held it as though swimming underwater.

"You're next, Mr. Wood," Candice Knott said. She dipped her scissors in clear blue fluid and dried them on a towel. She shook snippings of Chester Ford's hair from her barber cloth. Warm, fresh smells filled the place, all aftershave, hair cream, and talcum powder.

Lori Wood had always cut Alton's hair, ever since they first married. She'd clip it in the kitchen on the first Friday of each month. After she left, he'd let it grow. Before long, people started remarking about his hair. Was this, they asked, his new look? Such notice made Wood uncomfortable. So he'd started coming to Quick Clips on first Fridays. Then he switched to every second Friday. Haircut days were marked on his kitchen calendar now, scheduled through December.

Candice Knott had been his student five short years ago, pregnant during the spring term, by graduation obviously so. He'd always felt sorry for her, in a paternal sort of way. There was something about how her mouth was made, how her full lips never closed over her prominent teeth. She was perky and chatty all the same, her interest in science as fleeting as the snap of her bubble gum. *She does not apply herself.* He'd written this on Candice's report card, as he had on many others. Still, an active brain was at work, he'd felt certain, beneath her bright explosion of hair, behind her sadly malformed mouth.

Some days she'd bring her son to the shop. He'd play at the back of the room, where she'd strung a bright yellow plastic play-fence. The boy built towers with blocks and knocked them down with violent delight. Blocks scattered everywhere. Each time he'd survey the destruction he'd wrought, studying the scattered blocks like a riddle. Then he'd rebuild and do it again. This unvarying routine seemed bizarre to Wood and quite immature for the boy, who must now be almost five.

"Wash and clip, Mr. Wood?" Candice asked.

He nodded, and as he sat, he saw a small pocketknife wedged in the crease of the chair. She draped the cutting cloth over him, and he thought to say something about the knife, which he now clasped in his hand. She wrapped his neck with a crisp paper strip, all the while telling him of the rain that was predicted, how needed it was. The knife felt solid in his hand. It felt right, this small knife nestled there, this small and precious thing the world somehow wanted to be his. It was the kind he might have bought Logan one day, if his son had lived. Just for the moment he'd hold on to it, hold it and say nothing.

In the mirror he watched as Candice ran a comb through his hair, which looked thin in the shop's harsh light. It wasn't fast-growing or especially thick. Sometimes the girl's scissors snipped more air than hair. Wood enjoyed these visits though. He liked the feel of her hands lathering his scalp. She'd guide his head, tilt him back to the sink, and spray his hair, the tepid water rinsing the suds away. She'd towel his head, towel it like a wet dog, and he'd feel her strong fingers through the towel, feel in his scalp a rising of blood, a warmth like desire. As she cut his hair, he'd sit as if meditating, his gaze fixed. He'd watch Candice separate plaits of hair, clamp them between fingers, snip the ends. On his neck he'd feel her bubble-gum breath. He'd hear its seashell sound, her exhalations like a lover's in his ear.

Had one other person, he wondered, in the last two weeks touched him? Or had he been, however inadvertently, faithful again to the carefree girl he paid to cut his hair?

All this was pathetic. He knew that. He was pathetic. But it wasn't his fault. The fault of the matter resided in Lori. In Lori and the scraggy mechanic who'd lured her away. Wood was still pondering this—the pathetic nature of his situation, the pervasiveness of his departed wife's guilt—as he took his sport coat from the wall hook, and Candice, smiling in her toothy way, shook his hair from the cutting cloth. As he paid her, he could feel the penknife, which at some point he'd slipped into his pocket.

As promised, Alton drove. One thing Fran had come to rely on was her brother's predictability. He arrived outside her cottage five minutes early. She'd been waiting on the porch in her newest dress, one that fit her sturdy new size, waiting for fifteen minutes, checking her watch. The cats were all locked in the house. She'd counted them twice to be sure. There was extra food in their bowls, fresh litter in their boxes. After a day of heat, a light drizzle fell. It gathered mistlike on the maple leaves overhanging the porch, accumulated at green points, dripped free, and fell to earth. Fat drops splatted in the mud. As she waited, Fran had felt herself falter, suddenly uncertain. Had she remembered the right time, the right day? Alton arrived though. As she raised her umbrella and stepped off the porch, she could finally exhale, could finally relax.

Through the basement windows of Spivey Independent Christian Church, she saw pink and blue crepe-paper streamers. Inside, helium balloons dangling curly streamers danced across the low ceiling. It looked like a child's birthday party. This surely wasn't what Alton had in mind, bringing her along. Fran laughed at nothing. She laughed to be laughing. Deep in the room, music played. Olivia Newton-John sang a mellow song, a familiar one, from a record Fran had once owned. The room was crowded with people, their glances quick and away.

She tugged her brother's sleeve. "Loosen up," she whispered, as much to herself as to him. "Have some fun."

"Tickets?" Teresa Click asked.

Alton fished them from his wallet.

Teresa punched both and handed them back. "Hold on to them," she said. "I'm drawing stubs for a free Myrtle Beach couple's weekend at ten."

Fran certainly wouldn't go if she won. She hated the thought of the ocean, of so much water, miles of it, waves like whales rolling over, water dark and deep out to the horizon, children romping so mindlessly along the shore.

It wasn't just the ocean. She'd understand if it were. Lately, Fran couldn't go anywhere, not to the mountains, not to any distant place. If she left town, she imagined fire in her house, imagined broken water lines flooding her floors, freak storms uprooting trees that crashed through her roof. Or she'd imagine pet thieves breaking locks to kidnap her cats, selling them for medical research, selling them to foreign restaurants that skinned them and cooked them in exotic meat dishes. She'd read about it, pets disappearing while their owners were looking away. Some people refused to believe these stories. Alton, for example. But that didn't make them untrue. Fran knew that. Whether you believe something or not didn't really matter. Bad things happened to skeptical people too.

"Who'd you take," she asked Alton as they crossed the vacant center of the floor, "if Teresa draws your ticket number?" People clustered against the walls, their voices jovial in what seemed a forced way.

"The odds against my number being called," he answered, "are huge. And who says I have to take anyone? If you won't go . . ." He regarded her, waiting for her to answer what he hadn't asked.

"No," she said firmly.

"Who says I can't go alone," he asked, "on their Myrtle Beach weekend for two?"

Her face brightened. "And meet someone there?"

"Now that's a hyper-improbability."

"Have a little faith. Put yourself in position."

"Not yet," he said.

The music changed, the speakers too loud now for the next song that played. Shawn Colvin strummed hard on her guitar and sang angry lyrics about burning down a house. Fran felt a jittery rush. She imagined her house on fire, cats trapped inside. She imagined them racing room to room trailing flames.

Alton saw her wobble. He took her arm, and together they settled on folding chairs. For several minutes he held his sister's hand, patted it until he felt the trembling, which had come on her so suddenly, at last abate.

His long-absent wife, Lori, would never have understood this. And Wood could never explain it to her. In truth, sometimes it tore at him too. She'd accuse him of some strange complicity, of not caring enough, of gross insensitivity to her loss. She might repeat again what she'd often said, that no man who behaved that way could claim he loved his son. How could he argue that?

"Whatever demons visit Fran," Lori had told him in the weeks after the funeral, "they're earned. It's not the Lord's justice, not yet. That's still coming. But it's a righteous thing, what's happening to Fran. Don't you ever expect me to feel sorry for her."

Even though Lori was gone now, the vapors of her anger lingered, as persistent as her stale cigarette smoke in the curtains, in his car, in the fabric of old coats hanging deep in their closet.

Fran tried to pull her hand away and started to stand. "I shouldn't have come."

"It's okay," Wood said, holding on. "It'll be okay."

The music had changed again—a Beatles song now, "Penny Lane," its sprightly chorus of trumpets filling the air. Wood bounced his knee and their clasped hands in time with the tune. As he did, he saw, in the underarm of her dress sleeve, a price tag dangling from a plastic string. He took out the pocketknife, the one he'd found in the barber chair, and he showed it to Fran. The knife had pearly inlays and a single small blade, which was tarnished and dull. With it, he managed to cut the tag from Fran's dress, and she seemed to relax.

Wood went for drinks. As he crossed the floor, he was conscious of his clothes, how ridiculously inappropriate they seemed, his pale blue shirt, brown slacks, and tan loafers so priggish amid the sea of Key West shirts, bright skirts, and Capri pants. Even Brother Bob Fox, who ladled punch into red plastic cups, looked Caribbean in his nautical flag shirt, white crested blazer, and straw skimmer hat.

"My wife's secret recipe," Fox said. He flashed his trademark smile, all cheeks and teeth. "Orange-papaya-peach." Scoops of ice cream with cinnamon sticks jabbed through them floated in the punch like channel buoys.

"Two, please," Wood said. He grabbed a cookie, took a bite, brushed crumbs from his shirt. "I didn't realize it was a costume affair."

"Optional," Fox said. He glanced across to where his wife, Vickie Lynn, sat nearby. She wore a small circle of red roses. It floated like a memorial wreath on the bodice of her sea-foam dress. She returned the look, something coded between them.

Fox took the skimmer hat from his head and put it on Wood. The fit was loose, the top balanced on the crown of his head. "A costume," he said.

Wood handed it back. "Not quite." He made an effort to smile as he picked up the cups.

"Later tonight," Fox said, "a bunch of us are going to my place. We've got some cheeses, some wine to taste. We thought maybe you'd like to come."

Wood glanced around. No one seemed to be looking his way. Across the room, though, Donnie Slover had claimed the chair beside Fran. He was leaning close, whispering something to her.

"So, will you?" Fox asked. "Come?"

"Sure. Thanks," Wood said absently.

"Bring your sister too," Fox said.

"Right." He turned to leave. He felt marooned at the drink table now, paralyzed there, his chair beside his sister commandeered.

"We're sorry," Fox said, "about Logan."

Wood turned back toward the table, the cups like granite in his hands.

Fox gripped the brim of his hat. "So tragic."

"Yes. It was that."

"It's hard to see the Lord's hand, the divine purpose in such tragedy."

"Hard to see," Wood said. He turned the words over in his mind. "Over eleven thousand children drowned in the past decade, Brother Fox, the majority in swimming pools. Seventy-eight percent were boys. Look it up. It happens every day."

"I didn't mean—"

"If you discover that grand design, that divine purpose, you make sure it covers every last one of them. Them and my Logan too."

Fox leaned across the punch bowl. "I only meant that it's a mystery, things like that in this world. So tragic."

"Tragic," Wood said, and he turned again, determined now to get away from Fox, to deliver Fran's punch as he'd promised, to do at least that small thing.

Lori had needed a reason too, something solid to believe when their son drowned. She wanted a righteous God with good reasons. Or she wanted a villain to hate with the last remnant of her heart. Or better yet, she'd take both, bounce between the two until exhaustion drained the pain. Wood couldn't give her any of these. All he could offer, driving home from the cemetery, were statistics, probabilities, the verifiable numerical boundaries of uncertainty and fate.

"So cold," she'd said, her anguish overflowing. "You and your sterile statistics."

When he'd pulled over and tried to hold her, she'd pounded with the heels of her hands, her fists too tiny to bruise his chest. Beneath the overpass, she'd raked his neck with fingernails, and when blood came, she'd touched it, studied it on her fingers, seemingly amazed that something so crimson flowed in him.

Two days later Sheriff Tate summoned Alton to his basement office, along with Lori and Fran. Tate was a tall man, who looked folded up behind his desk, his shoulders hunched over, his knees bent at sharp angles. He had paperwork to complete, he told them, an inconclusive report from the county coroner to gather some facts around. Certain forms for the state, he said, must be completed.

Tate caught sight of Alton's neck bandage then, and he asked questions. He asked him to open the bandage, and when he did, Tate's deputy took photographs of the scratches and measurements, treating them like clues. He did all this even after Lori swore that she was the one who'd scratched her husband's neck, that it had happened quite accidentally the day of the funeral.

"Why aren't you questioning her?" Lori asked, and she pointed across at Fran. "Ask her how she let this happen. She said she'd watch Logan. We thought she'd keep him safe. Why don't you ask her?"

Tate did ask Fran, of course. That was his job. And she told him, her monotone echoing from some stony place inside, about watching Logan that day, about playing with the boy in Wood's backyard. His parents had shopping to do, she said, his birthday party to arrange, an early movie at the mall, a quiet restaurant meal. Fran told about raking leaves. She talked with a hand near her heart as if testifying. She described the blue plastic wading pool, its bottom layered with slick, black leaves, a season's accumulation of rainwater there. She told how the phone had rung and she'd rushed inside to answer because that's what she always did, answer ringing phones. And when she heard her brother Alton on the line, she'd assured him that everything was fine there, which it was. She'd zipped Logan into his plump winter coat, and he was raking leaves out back. The boy had tossed aside his toy rake and was raking up piles with the bamboo rake, the one his father used. And when she had gone to hang up, Fran said, Alton had asked her to wait.

Fran's voice grew hushed. Tate leaned closer, his forearms and hands on the papers spread across his desk. Lori lit another cigarette with jittery hands and blew smoke at the ceiling.

Alton had wanted, Fran said, to tell her before she hung up, to make sure she understood, that Lori's anger that morning was nothing personal, that his wife had been stressed and saying things she'd probably regret in a day or two. So they'd talked about that on the phone, cruel words that morning, talked too long about it, Fran said, her face red now and wet with tears.

Tate wrote something. As he stood and gathered papers, he glanced up at the wall clock. How long exactly, he asked, had they talked on the phone? How many minutes was Logan alone in the yard?

Fran held up her hands, her fingers splayed. "Ten?" She said it like a question, her voice weak, this answer only God could know. Her hands turned over, beseeched the ceiling, and then slowly settled back on her lap.

Tate shoved the papers into a large envelope and came around the desk to where they were sitting, waiting. "Sorry you folks had to come down here for this. It's state law." He took his hat down from its wooden wall knob and then turned back to them. "I know this ain't nothing but one untelling sorrow for the three of you."

Alton Wood danced twice that evening in the basement of Spivey Independent Christian Church. The first was a stumbling tour with Teresa Click, who seemed determined to dance at least once with every man there. A couple of women too. The other was a chain dance, a bunny hop, led by Bob and Vickie Lynn Fox, the couple who, although married, seemed somehow in charge of this singles mixer. Alton Wood chained in behind Clover McCoy. The lingering scent of lilac water and the woman's doughy waist beneath his hands drove him, as soon as the music ended, out the back door. He stood beneath the roof overhang. Men clustered there out of the drizzly rain. Silently they smoked.

Fran danced often, mostly with Donnie Slover. Shortly before ten o'clock, she whispered to Wood that she'd be riding in Donnie's pickup to Brother Fox's wine tasting. Donnie would be taking her home afterward too. "Don't feel like you have to come."

"I am tired," Wood said.

"Stop by my place?" she whispered. "Check on the cats?"

Wood found himself angry with her, angry at the brightness that seemed to fill her. Wasn't that what he'd wanted for her, why he'd asked her to come? But now that he saw her that way, he felt a curdling inside. He looked at his watch. He thought he might leave, check his sister's cats, and then call it a night. No mystery woman had made her move, nor was one likely to. He'd have left then, had it not been for Teresa Click, her fishbowl, the drawing.

The Myrtle Beach weekend for two went to Smith Hester, who owned Hester Tire and Transmission north of town. Hester, a foot-washing Baptist, wasn't there, couldn't be there, of course. His church was outspoken on the evils of dance. The fact that Hester had never set foot inside Spivey Independent Christian Church gave rise to grumbling among the gathered singles.

"It's for charity," Teresa Click said over the din. "The man paid for his tickets." She showed the signed stub she'd pulled from the fishbowl and held it up for the skeptics to see.

Wood felt a tingle of chagrin. He'd never had a chance of winning that trip. How could he have imagined otherwise? It went to the one who bought the winning ticket, the one who signed the stub.

Clover McCoy was beside Wood, her lilac scent stronger now. She leaned close and read the name for herself, hissed it like a curse, and ripped her ticket. "What are the odds?"

Wood could figure the odds, the probabilities. At that moment, though, it seemed a waste of his attention. Instead, he went to the fishbowl, which Teresa Click had tucked again beneath the crepe paper–draped table. He dumped the contents and spread the stubs across the table like pieces of a jigsaw puzzle, turning them over so the numbers and ink signatures showed. Several were written in turquoise ink. He read the name on the first, and he knew even before he matched the stub number with the ticket in his pocket, knew with certainty who'd sent his tickets.

On Monday morning, Alton Wood watched as Candice Knott, shifting bundles in her arms, unlocked the front door of Quick Clips. He hurried to help, taking the bundle of towels from her, carrying them inside when she'd opened the door. She pulled the keys from the lock. "Thanks," she said.

He took the knife from his pocket. "I found this," he said, "Friday, when I was here. I thought it was mine, but it wasn't."

"Ah," she said, taking it from his hand. "Chester Ford came back looking for this."

"It's like mine," Wood said. "It's not, though. It just looks the same."

Candice broke the string on the towels and stowed them on a shelf behind her chair. "He'll be thrilled to have it back."

"Good," he said. He turned toward the door and started to leave. But a question still niggled his mind, and he turned back again. "You sent me tickets in the mail?" he said. "The Independent Christian Church mixer?"

"You went?" she said. "Good."

"My sister had a better time," he said.

Candice sprayed a dust rag and ran it along the shelf, moving bottles, wiping away the thin layer of settled talc. "Then I'm happy for her," she said.

"What I'm wondering," he said, "I'm wondering why you sent them to me."

She stopped her dusting, opened the rag, and carefully re-folded it. "Sometimes you look so lonely," she said. "I feel sorry for you. I don't know. You seem so sad."

"Logan died," he said. "He's my son. And then my wife . . ." His hand flailed in the air like paper.

"I know," she said. "You hear stuff here." She started to wipe the back of her chair, the arms. "Anyway, I really wanted to win that Myrtle Beach trip for my boy, Brady, and me. I sealed the envelope, and he stuck the stamp on for luck."

"Smith Hester won."

"I didn't really expect to," Candice said. "We had fun, pre-tending we might."

"Odds are lousy," Wood said. He knelt and retrieved a toy building block from beneath a chair, turned it over in his hands, and then put it inside the plastic play-fence.

"Brady's never been there, never seen the ocean."

"Someday." He tried to make his voice hopeful, optimistic.

"I try to tell him about the ocean," she said, "but he doesn't understand. He can't, not until he's there for real."

"You'll take your boy," Wood said. "His name is Brady?"

She nodded. "He thinks the beach is like his sandbox," she said. "I took him to Lake Cumberland, took him swimming there. It's nothing like an ocean though. It's nothing like the sea."

"It's more," he said, "this massive thing. Way out in every direction. Rolling and deep. You're right. The boy can't comprehend, not without being there."

"I'm saving up," Candice said. She ran water in the sink and squeezed out the rag. "Can I ask about Logan?"

He didn't answer, couldn't answer.

"I don't want to make you sad," she said, looking at him in the mirror.

Wood checked his watch, the numbers there. He had to be at school soon, his first class of the day. If he left now, there'd be plenty of time. There'd be enough even if he got delayed, if something unexpected happened on the way.

Angel, His Rabbit, and Kyle McKell

The day Angel brought that damn rabbit home, I told myself it was nothing to get upset about. I told myself it was just this minor, annoying thing. I'd been around long enough to know that's how boyfriends can be—annoying—especially once they've moved in. This time I wanted things to be different. I wanted Angel to stay. I'd try hard to tolerate his ways, because, honestly, Angel's got so many good qualities. Putting up with things, I'd decided, was better than always getting into it. Getting into it is what my mother would do.

Anyway, about Angel's rabbit. He called it Victor. He told me it was a show rabbit, a champion of some kind. He said it had pedigrees, said I could shoot pictures if I wanted. At first he claimed to be keeping the rabbit for some friend. Before long, he was calling it collateral. He was holding on to the rabbit until this friend paid back what he owed. After a week, he brought Victor's cage onto the mud porch. These arrangements, he promised, were temporary. Every time Angel opened his mouth, another version of things came tumbling out. Looking back, I'm guessing he owned that rabbit all along.

"We'll get him some females," he said after the second week. "They'll breed. It'll be our business enterprise."

I told him this girl's life was plenty full without that.

"They'll have Victor's bunnies," he said, not giving up. "They'll be purebreds too. They'll be valuable." He got out paper and pencil. He wrote figures, erased, wrote some more. Then he slapped the pencil down, and he smiled over at me. Angel's dimples just melt my heart.

He held up the numbers. "Every twelve weeks," he said, "we'll double our money." I told him again it wasn't for me.

Understand. This rabbit, Victor, was nothing like what you'd think of as a real rabbit, the kind you see running wild. He wasn't the usual tame kind either, not one you'd give a kid for Easter. He was huge, the size of a boar raccoon, much too big for holding on your lap and way too skittish to pet. More than once I tried. His teeth could take your finger at the second knuckle. There's nothing you can do with a rabbit like that. So Angel kept Victor in that wire cage out on the mud porch. Day after day the rabbit sat out there, staring at my boots.

Maybe it's because Angel's got that name that he thinks he can do no wrong. Down at Gilly's Gas-N-Go, where he works, Juanita and Holly pronounce his name "on-hell," which is what I call him too, all *chica*-like, every time he gets puffed-up and full of his macho self, which he does way too often.

How many times I told Angel to burn the pissy newspapers and empty the turds piling up in the tray under Victor's cage, I can't say. Twenty times. Probably more. Maybe you think, when I noticed them piling up, I should've done it myself, which is what Angel finally said for me to do—empty the tray and burn the newspapers—instead of hassling him. But here's how I see things: this place might not be a mansion, but it's mine. I hold clear title to it and to the acre and three-quarters it sits on. That's no small thing in this world. I've got a paying job at the mall camera store, and I'm learning a profession, which is more than I can say for some. Every day I show up for work, even times I don't always feel like it. More to the point, this rabbit I'm telling you about is Angel's, and that makes the turds his too. That's how I think, and that's what I told him.

"If you feel that way, I'll get rid of him, sell him right now," Angel said. He tried to look pitiful. He stuck his fingers between the cage wires to scratch behind the rabbit's ears. It was the first time I'd seen him try that. Victor crouched to get away from him.

It was late on a Saturday afternoon. I was just home from work. I needed a warm shower and a cold beer. I didn't need this.

"Someone will buy him," Angel said. "You'll see. They'll gut him and skin him, cut him up for rabbit stew." He glanced over like he expected me to care. You could tell he was bluffing.

"Go ahead," I said. With my hands I made a gesture like wringing a neck. Maybe I bulged my eyes out too. That really set him off. When we get into it, I can't hold back. Neither can he. Holly says we're too much alike to last.

Angel slammed out of the house. Even Victor jumped at the noise, and he got all agitated and twitchy for a minute in his cage.

You can call me heartless too, call me a bitch like he did. I don't care. Sometimes a bitch is not a bad thing to be. Anyway, I'm just saying straight out how things were that day with my boyfriend and his damn rabbit, which, by the way, he didn't bother taking when he climbed into his pickup and sped off.

Twenty minutes later I was drying myself outside the shower stall when Kyle McKell called. I'd heard he was due back from the army any day, and here he was, just home and calling me.

"Dempsie," he said, "I'm coming over."

Everyone in town knew about the leg he'd lost fighting in Iraq. The story was in all the newspapers. So even though Holly and I had plans to go dancing that night, I told Kyle, "Come ahead."

"Get out those pictures you took," he said and hung up.

The pictures he meant were from five years ago. You might say they're what got me my job at McKell's Camera Outlet. It's nothing I ever talk about though. And by keeping that whole episode secret, I'd almost forgotten it myself.

Right away I called and canceled plans with Holly. I didn't say why, which probably misled her into thinking Angel was responsible. Then I started rummaging through drawers, looking for where I'd hidden those photographs.

While I searched, I couldn't stop thinking about Kyle's lost leg and the three steps he'd have to climb to my front door. Somehow I imagined him showing up in a neat khaki uniform with medals on his chest. He'd have an empty pant leg pinned up and wood crutches jammed under his armpits. It'd be a scene from a movie.

I had found the pictures and was sorting them on the bed when I heard a motorcycle rumble to a stop out front. The engine revved and shut off. Through the split in the bedroom curtains, I saw Kyle climb off the bike. He turned the bill of his ball cap from back to front. From behind a saddlebag, he unhooked a black walking cane.

Kyle's pant leg was definitely not pinned up. In fact, he walked on two legs, walked with a rolling kind of gait. If you didn't know Kyle McKell from before, if you hadn't seen how he was then, all agile and athletic, you might think he was just bruised up a little. You might think he'd turned an ankle or twisted a knee, judging by how he walked. You'd never suspect that one of his natural legs was gone.

By the time I got to the front door and opened it, he had his fist up and ready to knock. "Kyle," I said, going out. I hugged him carefully, not knowing what still might hurt. His balance wavered for a second, which made him hold me even tighter. His clothes smelled musty, like they'd been in his parents' basement too long.

"Hey, Dempsie," he said in my hair. My name sounded good coming from him.

Dempsie is what almost everyone calls me. It's okay as names go. It's nothing you'd want painted on an overpass though. It's actually my last name. Ashley, my first name, is way too common for anyone to use, anyone except my mother, that is. She never calls me Dempsie. Never. Dempsie is my father's name, after all, a name she swears will never pass her lips again, never in this lifetime. She thrives on bitterness. "Besides," she says, "what kind of name is that for a young woman when she's already got two sweet names like Ashley Lynn?" Most of the time I answer the phone when she calls. I just listen though. I quit arguing years ago.

Kyle seemed taller. Broader too. He isn't hard to look at, but he isn't what you'd call handsome either. He has too much nose and not enough chin, which means he photographs best straight on. His face seemed more sculpted, at his cheeks and around those hazel-brown eyes. It gave his face a more purposeful look. He tucked the ball cap into his waistband coming into the house. With a few finger-flicks, his corn-silk hair fell into place, neatly mussed. Beneath his dark gray jacket, Kyle wore a steel blue shirt. His shiny black sweatpants whispered as he walked. They gleamed too, with snaps and zippers everywhere.

I cleared Angel's three Oaxacan pillows off the couch so Kyle could sit, and I went to the kitchen for beers. When I got back, he had the jacket off, and he was rolling up a shirtsleeve. His left forearm had a strange shape. Angry scars, red raised ones, branched up it like rivers. "I wanted to show you this first," he said, "and skip all the awkward talk."

"Ouch," I said without meaning to. I sucked air between my teeth. You could still see the surgeon's stitch pattern. Stray black hairs sprouted up in odd places. He raised the arm and showed the other side. The skin was a patchwork, some tanned, some pale blue and veiny, like the sides of a newborn's head.

I was holding the bottles—Negra Modelo and Bud Light—that I'd brought from the kitchen. I gave Kyle his choice. He took the Mexican beer, sipped, and seemed pleased. He turned the fat bottle in his hands, reading the gold label or pretending to. The writing was all Spanish.

I piled two pillows on the floor and sat. "Does it hurt?" I asked.

"The arm?" He shook his head. "Not like the leg."

I'd almost forgotten the leg. I wondered how much was gone.

Kyle kept studying the bottle. "The arm's got a permanent ache," he said, "deep in the bones. You know what I mean?"

I couldn't imagine. For some weird reason, I wanted to touch that arm.

"They tell me the pain goes away," he said. He smiled as if there was something funny about that.

"Three times a week I get physical therapy," he said. "Exercises." He moved his arm, cranked it like something mechanical. Then he let the arm rest on the knee of the leg that must have been artificial. That ankle beneath his pant leg was fat as a softball. Kyle made a fist with his hand and he squeezed an imaginary rubber ball. The arm muscles slithered under the patched-up skin.

I had to look away. I made myself look away, and when I did, I wanted to look back again, wanted to look closer. A shudder ran up my back. This wasn't like I'd expected.

"It's okay, Dempsie," Kyle said. "It's nothing I like seeing either."

"I'm sorry," I said. I truly was. I felt his hand on my quivering knee.

I got to my feet, and the hand fell away.

"I'm the same person," he said. "Just look at me. That's all I'm asking. Just look."

I picked up my beer and backed away. "I'll go get the pictures you wanted," I said.

"Just look," Kyle said again. "Don't walk away. You owe me that much."

He was right, of course. I did owe Kyle McKell.

I crossed the room to the couch again, set my beer on the table, and sat beside him.

When you're young, you do stupid stuff. I know I did, lots of it. This one time, Ashleigh Tinker and I hatched a plan to steal a camera to take on our senior class trip. We'd be going to Washington DC, staying at a hotel five days. It would take every bit of my savings. We wanted pictures of monuments and museums, not just postcards but pictures we were in. There'd be partying at the hotel too, which was another reason we needed that camera. We intended to make memories, ones we'd treasure forever. We wanted a real camera, not the drugstore cardboard kind or a cheap plastic one like my mother's, which you couldn't even find film for anymore. I wanted a quality camera. I wanted one bad. And the more I thought about wanting one, the worse the wanting got.

Tinker and I downed whiskey shots out in her father's toolshed to calm our nerves. We rolled a joint from the old man's weed scraps, and together we smoked it down to the pinch. By the time we got to the mall, we were way calm.

Kyle McKell, whose father managed the store, sat on a stool behind a glass counter. He was reading a magazine, which he slapped closed and tucked away when I went in.

"Hey, Dempsie," he said. I remember being amazed that he knew my name.

I started chatting with him. I told him about our class trip. I leaned across the display case, looked in, and pointed at different cameras. I asked him about the Minoltas and Nikons, about lenses and different kinds of film. Every time I'd point at a camera, Kyle would bring it out. He seemed friendlier than I remembered from school, more relaxed. He let me handle the cameras, let me get the feel of them, let me see each one up close. Before long, we must have had a dozen spread out.

"Someday," I said, "I'd love to work in a camera store." I framed his face in a viewfinder and clicked the shutter. Even without film, it felt real. "I might study photography too," I told him, "and own cameras like these." Just saying something out loud can make it seem possible.

Kyle looked toward the front of the store and then back at me. "Really?" His voice sounded husky now.

"No lie," I said. It felt risky, revealing dreams in the middle of so much deceit. But he had kind eyes, and that's what I did.

While he was busy with me, Tinker was supposed to wander in. She'd find the best display camera, something compact, and slip it into her shoulder bag. She'd signal with a cough and then leave. That was the plan. It was a good plan too, one that had worked in other stores for cosmetics.

Kyle glanced toward the front again. I looked too. We were still alone. He put the camera down. "Wait here, Dempsie," he said. "Mine's in the office, a Pentax. You think you could handle it?" He started for the back of the store without waiting for my answer.

Opportunity doesn't always bother with knocking. Sometimes it just throws open the door.

As soon as Kyle disappeared behind the office curtain, I grabbed the compact Nikon and slipped it into my bag. I went around the counter and snatched the empty box too, then hurried back to where I'd been. When he came back with his camera, I was fiddling with the bulky Minolta's lens, really studying the settings.

The expression on Kyle's face wasn't so relaxed now. He looked toward the front door once more. Everything inside me pulled tight.

"You picked a good one, Dempsie," he said, "that Nikon." He pointed to where the camera had been.

I straightened, stepped back, groping in my mind for some way to deny it. There was no way, though, and I knew it. My insides sank. I took the box and camera from my bag and put them with the others on the counter. "It's back," I told him. "I put it back."

"No harm, no foul?" Kyle said. His eyes were hard to read.

"Nothing happened," I told him. I wasn't far from tears, which I did not want him to know. "You've got your camera back."

He fitted the Nikon into its box and put the cover on. "It's not my camera," he said. He slid it back across the counter. He busied himself putting the others away, then took up the Pentax again. "This is my camera, Dempsie. Everything else here," he said, "it's just merchandise."

I looked at the box, looked at Kyle, looked at the box again, waiting for him to say clearly what was going on. You could tell he was turning something over in his mind.

Just then I heard Tinker's fake cough. With everything going on, she'd come in without my noticing. Kyle didn't seem to have noticed her either. Even after the fake cough, he didn't so much as glance her way.

He said, "You want the Nikon?" His face told me nothing.

I reached for the box, but Kyle grabbed it first. "What?" I asked.

He let go, took his hand away. It trembled a bit, retreating. "It's yours," he said, "if you do me a favor."

I looked around the store for Tinker. She was nowhere to be seen.

"Shoot some pictures," he said. "Shoot pictures of me. That's all I'm asking." His voice trembled now too. "Have them developed while you're in DC."

I picked up the box, the Nikon inside. Confusion swirled in my head.

"Please?" he said.

When I still didn't answer, Kyle reached for the magazine he'd tucked away. He opened it on the counter and turned it to face me. He flipped pages, showing me what he had in mind.

The photos Kyle wanted me to take that night weren't the kind he'd want his parents to see. They weren't what he'd want anyone in Burkitt County to see. Maybe not in the whole state. The photos were for his friend, Dwight Poole. Poole had moved that month to Chicago, joining a dance company there. Kyle explained all this later that night, explained it as I hesitated outside the room he'd rented at Motel 6. I told myself I could still change my mind.

"I'm gay," he said, as if I hadn't figured it out from the magazine he'd showed me that afternoon. "You're in no danger here."

"I know," I said. Still, I didn't budge. It felt dangerous, being anyplace with him.

There was a frustrated look on Kyle's face. "Please, Dempsie?"

he said. He took the key card from his pocket. "Please don't make this so hard."

He slipped the card into the lock slot and pulled it out. The lights flashed green on the first try, which I took as a positive sign.

Tinker and I each had our own cameras for the DC trip. I brought enough film for both of us, even though her camera turned out to be digital. The first day there, I took Kyle's four secret rolls for developing at a pharmacy on Rhode Island Avenue. On the film envelope I checked the boxes for double jumbo prints and glossy. I made up a name and address for the yellow envelopes. Two days later, when the clerk handed me the photo packets, her undisturbed face told me she hadn't peeked inside. I paid and left the store. When I felt certain that no one was following, I opened the envelopes and looked.

I liked what I saw, these posed photos of Kyle, the way the light looked on his skin, the deep shadows and subtle colors. Everything looked more real in the photos, looked more vivid than it had that night. The photos seemed somehow precious—artistic, in a way—like paintings. Artistic. It's a way I hadn't seen myself before.

You might wonder why I ordered double prints. I could say I just checked the box because it was there. That wouldn't be a lie. I could say that I wanted an extra set to be safe, that I didn't totally trust Kyle about letting me take something valuable like that camera, no strings. That's what I told him about the double prints, and there's more than a little truth in it. I could tell you that I wanted copies because I realized, even then, that Kyle's motel photo session could be a start for me in photography, that I wanted to remember that as much as the DC trip. That would be true too. Sometimes life offers a person way more reasons than they need.

I sat beside Kyle on the couch and let him show me his injured arm. He talked about the attachments, the muscles and nerves involved, the finger numbness, all the ligament damage. I tried not to be squeamish. He traced things with his finger as if he could see inside. He kept talking about that injured arm in expert ways. He knew how it all worked together. He knew it the way Angel knew cars.

"My father wants to hear nothing about wounds," Kyle said. "He wants to hear about good deeds, what he thinks I was doing there. My mother leaves the room if I even mention the arm."

"Or the leg?" I was more than a little curious about that.

He finished his beer. "She can't handle any of it," he said, handing me the empty.

I was in the kitchen getting him another beer from the refrigerator when Angel came in the back door. "Whose Harley's out front?" he asked, easing the door closed.

"You're back," I said. I wished he wasn't.

"Maybe," Angel said and shrugged. He wasn't over it yet either. "Who's here?"

"My boss's son," I told him. "Kyle."

"The wounded one?" Angel asked. I nodded. He took the beer from my hand and popped the cap with his belt buckle. "He going to stay late?"

"Maybe." I shrugged. I could be that way too. Behind the milk, I found a carton of onion chip dip. It looked okay. Smelled okay too.

"You think he's something," Angel said. He wrapped me in his arms from behind, grabbed on to me like everything I've got belonged to him. He did it in a playful way, having decided by himself that it was time we made up. "You think this army man is the real deal," he said like a growl in my ear.

I jabbed with my elbows, jabbed hard and twisted free. "He lost his leg over there, Angel!" I tried to keep my voice down. "For Christ's sake!"

"*Dios mío!*" he gasped, staggered back in mock horror. "Then we must help him to find this lost leg, to find it before he falls over."

With my empty hand I swung at him. He was quick though, stepping back. Like a boxer, he feinted, slap-jabbed at me, danced away. "I float like the butterfly," Angel said. He shuffled his feet, circled across the linoleum. He could be such a *muchacho* at the worst times.

I put frozen pizza treats in the microwave, pressed buttons, and dumped potato chips into a bowl. "You joining us?" I asked.

"Three's a crowd," he said.

"Suit yourself," I said. I tried to mask my relief with another shrug.

Angel took the chip bowl from my arms, and he grinned. "I like crowds."

"You got nothing to worry about in there," I said. It was truer than he knew. I spread warm pizza treats on a plate and started collecting up everything—bowls, plates, and new beers.

From the cupboard, Angel grabbed his green hot sauce, the stuff he sprinkled on everything. "Bring napkins," he said, tucking the tiny bottle into a shirt pocket. "And relax, *chica*. You won't hardly know I'm there."

I grabbed napkins, and we went to the front room.

"Wow," Kyle said, seeing what Angel and I were bringing. We must have looked like old married hosts. It really wasn't much, just refrigerator and microwave food, and I told Kyle so.

"She's so modest," Kyle said, "this girlfriend of yours." He got up and stood long enough to shake Angel's hand.

"Dempsie? Modest?" Angel said. He sputtered a laugh.

"You know. Humble," Kyle said, sitting again. He put his cane on the floor. "About the food."

"I know the word," Angel said. "I spoke English since I was two." I hoped he'd quit right there. Not likely, I knew. He took his beer and some chips and went to sit in his favorite chair. It's off to one side, a plush chair with a side holster for the television remote.

Kyle tried the chip dip. "I'm just saying not everyone can put on a spread with no warning."

"My brothers and sisters, all of us, we're bilingual," Angel said. "That's what you'd call us if we were *anglo* anyway, bilingual, not ESL, which is what everyone wants to say because it's us."

I offered Kyle the pizza snacks. He took some on a napkin.

"I always dream in English," Angel said, "even back in Mexico."

"Strange," Kyle said. His interest seemed real.

Angel pulled the hot sauce bottle from his pocket and sprinkled his chips. "It wouldn't be my choice for dreaming," he said. "Spanish is better for everything but school. You can mean more, talking Spanish."

"Angel promises he'll teach me a little bit," I said. "*Un poquito.*" I'd already learned a few phrases.

"But then she will know all my secrets." Angel winked at Kyle. You'd think they were pals and I was just some girl. Angel leaned over the side of his chair and offered his bottle of hot sauce to Kyle, who took it.

"I learned some Arabic phrases," Kyle said. He put the sauce bottle on the table without using it. "They trained us how to give greetings in Iraq," he said, "using the right gestures so we wouldn't offend anyone. We learned to shout out these Arabic commands too, so the Iraqis would know what to do."

Angel came over and got another beer. "They say it's hot over there." He said it to Kyle like a question. He stole a quick look at Kyle's legs, glanced fast and then away. He couldn't help it either.

"Hotter than the hinges of Hades," Kyle said. You could tell by how quickly he said it that he'd said it a hundred times before.

"I can't stand summer heat," I said.

"Iraq heat is real heat, oven heat, all day and every day."

"You get used to it though," Angel said, standing there. "Right?"

"Not me. Some said they did, but I never believed them." We all drank from our bottles then, the three of us together, as if that Iraq heat had found its way into my place.

From the table, Angel grabbed up his little green bottle and went back to his chair. When the subject was heat, he'd usually say something about Mexico or August heat in tobacco fields he'd worked. Angel could get competitive about anything. He wasn't this time though. Instead, he asked, "How'd it happen, the leg? You get shot?"

"An explosion." Kyle said it like it was nothing.

"An IUD?" Angel asked.

"IED," I said.

"Probably a grenade," Kyle said, "something thrown." He shrugged again. This time I saw the tension in his shoulders, the strain on his face. He only wanted it to be nothing.

"We're patrolling like we do every day, five of us, and I'm telling Horton some dumb joke," he said. "In an instant, the world's upside down. I can't hear a thing. I see Horton not five feet away, and he's lying there all opened up like meat. I try to get up, to run with the others, and I'm totally pissed because the leg, which I don't know is gone, won't work."

"*Santa Maria,*" Angel said. He made the sign of the cross.

"Next thing I know, I'm in a hospital bed. Bags of fluid are draining into me, and some of it must be sedatives because the minute they tell me the leg's gone, my world goes white. I wake up in Germany."

"I'm sorry," I said. I put my hand on his good leg and then took it away. It was hard to know what to say or do. We ate and drank in silence, the three of us, for the longest time. All the while, you could hear the battery wall clock across the room tick off seconds.

"Dempsie," Kyle said at last, "how's your photography?"

I let out the breath I didn't know I'd been holding.

I brought out my portfolio and showed him my best nature photographs, my plant and horse and scenery photos, most of them taken within a mile or two of my place. The horses weren't thoroughbreds. They were regular horses, ones my neighbors kept and rode or just kept now that they were old.

On the television, Angel watched his Spanish cable channel, a variety program with an audience that was part of the show. Angel kept the volume low. On the show, a Mexican chef in a high white hat was giving lessons, cutting a whole watermelon to make a fancy basket of fruit and melon balls. A bikini model was his student. She wasn't acting very bright, making lots of mistakes. She tried to cut the melon with the dull side of her knife. Nobody could be that stupid. Skinned peaches slipped out of her hands. She kept licking juice from her fingers, laughing as she did. Before long her watermelon basket was a wet mess. She was too. She tried hard though, and the audience applauded and laughed. Angel, on his fourth beer, laughed too.

Kyle leafed back through my photography folio. He really looked at each print, the big ones and the small ones too. He asked questions. Sometimes he'd flip back to an earlier one, comparing it. When he finished, he closed the folio. "Now," he said quietly, "you've got some pictures for me?"

In my bedroom I gathered up the photos he wanted and the negatives too. I don't think they all got back into their original yellow packets or all the negatives and photos matched up. But it all was somewhere in the bundle I banded together.

When I got back to the front room, Angel had turned off the television. He was over by Kyle, in front of him, pointing the neck of his empty bottle at Kyle's legs, asking some question. Kyle didn't seem to mind. He reached down and unfastened snaps on his pant leg. He opened it halfway up to the knee, spread the pant leg wide.

Angel knelt, trying to get a better look. He didn't look very steady doing it.

Kyle's lower leg was a black pipe not too different from his cane. It looked like something a plumber might use. The pipe screwed into a ball-shaped ankle twice the size of a real one. An axle ran through the ankle, the fat ends coming out more or less where anklebones should be. The bottom third of the ball disappeared into Kyle's shoe, which I realized now wasn't any more Kyle's than the fake foot was. The shoe belonged to the machinery.

"There is a motor in there?" Angel asked.

"The ankle?" Kyle shook his head. "The only motor is in the knee." With his two hands, he flexed the foot and ankle, moving it like walking. "The ankle has hydraulics and springs inside," he said. "They adjust when my weight shifts." He pulled up on the toe of his shoe, and the ankle flexed. He let go, and the foot moved smoothly back straight.

Angel was sitting on the floor now. I could tell he wanted to see more. Kyle must have realized it too. He unfastened several more pant-leg snaps, exposing the knee hinge and some upper leg, a wide metal strut.

With a knuckle, Kyle tapped the shell covering the knee. It made the sound of an empty terrapin shell. "I'm still learning to use the new motor," he said. "It's experimental." With both hands he grasped the strut and lifted. The knee bent with a hushed, whirring noise. A small smile came across his face.

"That's the motor?" Angel said. He moved around to where the light was better.

"Quiet, ain't it?" Kyle said. "I feel it though, feel it like you wouldn't believe, this quiet hum and tiny ratchet clicks up in my hip." He moved the leg again and flexed the knee almost silently. The smile came back. I couldn't look away. I tried to imagine the sensations—the hum, the intimate clicks—tried to imagine feeling them deep in my own hip. For a moment, I thought I did.

"It's like you see in movies," Angel said, "people with robot parts." He opened another beer. "Fucking Schwarzenegger."

"Robocop," I said. "He's just movie CGI shit, all computer-faked stuff. This is real."

Angel looked over at me like he'd forgotten I was there. "What I'm saying is the idea's the same. The concept."

"They can fake anything in movies," I said. "This is fucking real."

"You want to see real?" Kyle said. Using his good leg, bracing his weight with an arm, he scooted awkwardly from the couch to the floor. He rolled onto his side and worked his pants waist down past his knees. Then he held his shirttail aside.

His shorts were this white elastic material, legless briefs, tight like cycling shorts. Several inches of leg stump showed, the skin red, the flesh lumpy. The stump disappeared into the fake leg's fitted leather boot. A crisscross harness strapped the thing in place like a jockey's saddle—one long diagonal strap to the opposite hip, a short strap to his groin, crossing an ugly scar there.

My insides clenched up. I had to look away.

He rolled onto his side. A braid of fine wires snaked up from the backside of the boot. Just above Kyle's waist, low on his back, the wires were taped to a wide blue tattoo. "My landscape, a nerve resection," he said, "a neural rerouting that works with my trusty computer chip."

He rolled back, cinched both straps tight, and then patted the side of the boot. "Computer chip's right here."

"Damn!" Angel said. He knelt close to look.

Kyle's hand moved to the front of the boot and lifted a leather flap. "Batteries included," he said, showing them. They looked like they belonged to a cell phone. With a finger he pried loose a fabric packet wedged beside the batteries. "Also convenient," he said, unrolling the fabric on the table, "for a private stash." He removed a fat joint and stuffed the packet back.

"Fuck, man," Angel said. He rocked back and laughed. "You're loving this too much." He slapped Kyle's good leg, slapped it like an old friend.

Kyle swung backhanded at him, swung hard, his fist thudding on Angel's chest. Angel lost his balance and fell back against a chair. "It's all fucking toys," Kyle said, biting on the words. "Nothing but bright, shiny toys."

"I didn't mean nothing." Angel stumbled to his feet. He looked at me like I should do something about it. "*Cabrón*," he muttered at Kyle, and he went to the kitchen.

The change in Kyle, his flash of rage from nowhere, had taken my breath. Now he worked his pants back up, bent, and snapped the pant leg. When he finally sat straight again, he looked over at me. There was a vacant look in his red-rimmed eyes, not at all like the eyes I remembered.

In my hands I saw the photo packets, the ones he'd come for. I held them out to him. He stared for several seconds, uncomprehending.

"From DC," I said.

He took them then and tucked them away in his pocketed pants. I wanted to tell him that I hadn't shown them to anyone, not even Angel, that I'd kept his secret and he had nothing to worry about. I wanted him to know that. I couldn't say any of it though.

Kyle worked himself up onto the couch again. He lit the joint, inhaled, and offered it to me. I took it, toked, and let the smoke settle deep in me before passing it back. It was the weekend, Saturday night, Sunday tomorrow. What the hell.

From the rear of the house, I heard loud banging and dull thuds, and I rushed to see. Angel had picked up the rabbit cage. He carried it now, staggered with it. He was trying to take the thing outside in the dark, trying to fit it crosswise through the porch doorway. I switched on the light. Inside the cage, Victor cowered, his eyes darting and panicky.

I pushed past Angel and propped the door open with a broom handle. "Turn sideways," I told him. The chill evening air was a splash on my face.

Angel made it through the doorway, bumped through, and managed to hit all three steps going down without falling. He lugged the cage out across the dark yard.

"What're you doing?" I yelled.

"Setting Victor free. You think I did something wrong," Angel yelled back. His breath puffed out, small alcohol fog-balls in the air. "I think this rabbit offends you by being here."

"Keep him, Angel," I yelled. "I don't care. Just clean up after him."

He set the cage down, unlatched and opened the door. Victor hunkered in a corner. Angel kicked the back of the cage. He kicked it again. He banged the top mesh and sides with his hands. Victor squeezed through the door opening and wriggled out. Once out, he hopped heavily across the yard, zigzagged into the darkness, and headed for the woods out back.

Angel came toward me, pushed past me onto the porch. He picked up the tray full of rabbit turds and took it out to the burn barrel. He dumped it there, a disgusting topping for yesterday's trash. Back on the porch, he gathered up the pissy newspapers, the other old newspapers stacked there, took them out, wadded them, and stuffed them into the burn barrel too. Then he touched a match to it all.

"It's best all around," I said. He might not have heard. I walked out to Angel. I put my arms around him and tried to kiss him. No way was he letting that happen. Not yet.

"He won't make it," Kyle said, coming out from the house, pinching the joint. How much he'd heard, I didn't know. "Tame rabbits won't survive in the wild."

"Big expert," Angel said. "He knows rabbits too."

Kyle came over by the fire. There wasn't much smoke, and what there was went straight up. The heat felt good on my face. "I raised rabbits years ago, dozens of rabbits," Kyle said. "They were a 4-H project." He extended the joint. Angel looked at it, thought for a second, and took it. "We sold them all for meat afterwards."

"You had them butchered?" I said. "That's so cruel."

"Set them free," Kyle said, "and they won't survive. They've got no immunities. They pick up parasites, all sorts of diseases. They're easy prey too, prey for coyotes, for foxes, even dogs."

Angel offered the joint back. Just that fast, you could see him mellow out.

Kyle waved it away. "Any more and I forget which legs are real."

Angel gave a laugh. "That one," he said, pointing like it was a guessing game, as if the guy could suddenly switch his fake leg. "Am I right?"

Kyle got a kick out of that. "They're both real," he said. "It's the third leg, the one that's gone but still feels real, that's the one that can screw you up."

"You still feel it?" I asked. My brain was slowing down.

"It's weird. Sometimes you forget. You think it's still there." He looked serious now. "It hurts like it's still there, and it itches sometimes—the knee, the ankle, the foot. It feels wet in the bathtub. Believe it's there at the wrong time though, and you'll fall flat."

"The leg is gone," Angel said, and he nodded. "Its soul remains." I thought about it for a minute, the idea of a leg's soul. It was a thought I liked thinking, something I could almost believe.

"It's all illusion though," Kyle said, as if he'd been thinking it too. "The doctors, they tell me it's a phantom in my head. It's all muscle memory and unconnected nerves firing like they've still got work to do."

Two or three streets away, a dog barked. Another answered from farther away.

"Dogs are everywhere in Fallujah," Kyle said, "dogs nobody owns anymore. They follow us on night patrols." He looked away. "We shoot the ones that bark."

Angel peered off into the darkness, stared out toward the woods. The trees looked ghostly in the dim moonlight. "Is that true?" he asked Kyle, "What you said before about rabbits set free, about coyotes and everything?"

"I'm afraid so," Kyle said.

Angel started walking away, heading out the woods path. "Victor," he called, as if that rabbit was some house pet. For the minute or two after he'd disappeared, you could hear Angel whistling too.

With a stick I turned the smoldering fire to make sure everything would burn. The smoke smelled like road tar.

Kyle unzipped a deep pocket, took out the yellow bundle, and moved closer to the fire. He opened the photo packets and started going through the photographs, looking at them. He fed one and then another into the flames. Dark ashes and bright embers rose up, drifted up like resurrection, vanishing in the night sky.

"You don't have to do that," I told him, reaching for the stack. "I didn't show anyone. I wouldn't."

He pulled away and kept at it, looking at each photo, dropping it in the barrel. One time he stopped and held up a photo for me to see. "You're good at this, Dempsie," he said. The one he held was my favorite too.

"Save it for me?" I wanted to beg. He could burn the others if he wanted. They were all his, after all. But why not let me have that one?

For a moment I thought he might. "I can't," Kyle said, and he let it fall.

After they all were in the fire, he dropped the negatives in too, the empty envelopes, the rubber bands that had held them together. He stepped back and turned away from the fire. "It's not that I didn't trust you," he said. "Besides, my parents already know how things are with me. I told them in the hospital."

"Then why?" I asked. "Why burn everything?"

Kyle tapped the shaft of his cane on the fake knee. "This is me now, someone with a wired-up tech-toy for a leg," he said. He hit the leg again, hit it harder. "This. It's who I've got to be from now on. The old Kyle McKell, the one in the pictures, the one with two good legs?" His hand fluttered up like one of the embers. "I'm better off forgetting."

We walked back to the house. As we did, I thought about Kyle, how he'd make a good boyfriend for me—an excellent one maybe—except for the part about being gay. If it weren't for that, I could imagine us as a couple, which is to say I really liked the guy. I could get used to his nose and chin. And Kyle, he definitely needed someone like me, especially now. Okay, it wouldn't work. I know that. But the thought definitely crossed my mind. Like a freight train, it crossed.

A million bugs swarmed the porch light. Kyle used his cane climbing the steps. I tried to help too. He went up without needing it though. You could hear his hum and clicks this time, such inhuman sounds coming from inside a man.

The idea arrived then that Angel must have thought all along that there was a secret connection between Kyle and me. I wanted to believe that he had, wanted to believe in the worst way. Imagine, mattering that much to someone.

In the corner of the porch, I saw a twitch, looked closer, and saw Victor. The rabbit was nestled against my boots. His eyes were on us. His ears lay flat against his head. He didn't look frightened now or excited in any way. Lying there with my boots, Angel's rabbit looked downright comfortable.

A Male Influence in the House

Robert slid a tampon from the box his mother kept beneath the bathroom sink. It seemed such a perfect thing, such a secret and mysterious thing, wrapped as it was in crisp white paper. There was a prickling sensation on the boy's skin and an energy he could hardly restrain in his fingers, his hands, the muscles of his legs. Behind his eyes, an urgent ache took hold.

The boy stood, and as he did, he glimpsed his pale reflection in the mirror. "What's your problem?" he asked. He wedged the tampon between two fingers like a fat cigarette and posed with it. "What?" he said, shoving his chin out. "You got a problem?" He mimed a puff and exhaled a long plume of imaginary smoke. "Tell me, douche bag," he said, glaring now, stabbing the thing at the mirror, "exactly *what* is your problem?"

The boy in the mirror stared back in what seemed to Robert a dim-witted way.

He pulled his gaze free. He straightened, made himself tall, and stuffed the tampon into a pocket. At the faucet he wet both hands and combed them through his hair. Turning away from the sink, he started to go and then jerked back to look again in the mirror. Just once he wanted to catch his reflection unaware, to see himself look even slightly away. *Not in this life,* he told himself. In the mirror, the boy's lips seemed to move with the words.

Robert's greyhound barked in its outdoor pen. It was a mournful, lonely sound to the boy, nothing like a real dog's bark. He went to the window, spread the curtains, and looked out. It was still early, too early for his mother, who was working full shifts at the factory this week, to be home. He checked the clock in the kitchen. Time was running short. In less than an hour her Harley would be pulling into the yard.

All day at school, Robert had bolstered himself with imaginings of his free hour. He'd made promises to himself, serious promises, ones that he intended to keep. Back at the sink, he knelt and checked beneath it again. Satisfied that nothing he'd touched looked disturbed, he stood again and left the bathroom without a glance back at the boy in the mirror.

Robert's uncle, Jerry, had given the aging greyhound to him in what seemed a kind of offering. That was three weeks ago, the morning that Jerry, after vanishing for several months, drove up in his battered GMC pickup, the terrified dog tethered by bailing twine in the truck's trash-heaped bed. The next day Jerry moved in with Robert and his mother.

"He's my brother after all," she told Robert, as if he didn't know what an uncle was. "Besides, you need a male influence," she said. "Jerry will have to do, at least for now."

Robert hadn't much liked the idea. He still didn't. The place seemed somehow trespassed upon with Jerry there, even if this was, as his mother had promised, just for the time being, just until Jerry found work and could afford a place of his own. In recent weeks, his mother had seemed happier. Robert had to admit that. She seemed cheerier, in fact, than he remembered her ever being. Maybe helping her brother was doing her good too. So Robert was trying to like the guy. He was really trying. And he was trying to like the gift greyhound too.

Jerry could drive up at any time. His schedule was erratic, and he'd come and go at odd hours, doing whatever he did all day. He said he had prospects. He said he knew people, said he had all sorts of connections. He had feelers out, he said, things brewing, lots of irons in the fire.

Robert jumped down from the porch, the screen door slamming behind him. The greyhound stood with its front paws high across the top of the wire mesh pen. Its stance looked painful and unsteady. The dog's coat was a drab charcoal color, the lower brisket and chest whitened with age. According to Jerry, its name was Marty. But the boy couldn't make himself call the dog that. Instead, he called it nothing.

Jerry said that he'd bought the dog—a purebred, he said, a retired racing champion—from the divorcing couple that lived a half mile through the woods and across Clear Creek. Robert had heard the talk about them. They'd built an enormous log house at the end of the petered-out road and lived there like lords. The house had acres of solar panels on the roof and a half dozen by-god windmills out back. They'd moved out, Jerry said, and had put the place up for sale. So he'd picked up Marty at a bargain price.

"Dog needs a home," he said. "Besides, taking care of a dog is good for a boy." Robert failed to see benefits as he fed the greyhound morning and night, as he walked it along the road, as he scooped ropy shit piles from the pen and carried them on the shovel blade to the edge of the woods to catapult away.

For the first week, he kept the dog tied to the white oak out back with a length of chain. The dog pulled against the end, though, and the boy worried about its neck. He tried loosening its collar. The next day the dog escaped, backing its sleek head out of the collar. Late that evening, Jerry found Marty back at the vacant log house, asleep on the back porch steps.

That weekend, Robert's mother helped him build a pen. They used rusted posts and bent-link fencing that Jerry had scavenged from somewhere. The pen was small, smaller than the boy's bedroom. The dog was off the chain, though, and Robert felt relieved about that. The dog would pace the pen perimeter. In the afternoon, it would sleep in the cool green shade of the nearby pear tree.

"Down," Robert said loudly as he approached the pen, pushing the palm of his hand at the dog. Marty got down and wagged his tucked tail. A younger dog could probably jump the fence without a running start. Marty seemed too tired though, too achy and old to even try.

The dog circled to the empty water bowl as Robert came near. The boy opened the gate and grabbed the bowl. At the house spigot, he filled it. *There's no time for this,* he told himself, *not now.* He set the bowl hurriedly inside the fence. Water sloshed out. "I'll feed you when I get back," the boy said. He patted the dog's flank while its tongue lapped water. Backing away, Robert closed the gate, latched it, and left.

He followed the path through the woods and down the rocky side slope. His breathing was shallow now. The air in his lungs felt urgent and alive. There was a frizz of anticipation in his limbs, an eagerness in his brain, an asphalt taste on his tongue. At the bottom of the slope, the path followed Clear Creek through a stand of trees to a shallow fording place. He crossed the stream there, leaping from rock to rock. On the other side, he clambered up the slope to a weedy backyard where the silent giant wind turbines stood and beyond them the vacant log house.

Even from the back, the place looked like a log-homes catalog photo. The logs themselves looked huge and freshly varnished. Solar panels on the roof gleamed with streaks of purple and gold beneath the late afternoon sun. Along the foundation, small evergreen plantings, roots cramped in burlap balls, were turning brown. Along the lip of the shake-shingled roof, copper gutters, their joints tinged around and streaked down in green, led to copper downspouts. Blue plastic rain barrels stood like sentinels along the back of the house.

Robert placed an overturned bucket under the garage window. He stepped up onto it and pulled himself onto the sill, just as he had several times before. He balanced there for a moment before tumbling through and easing himself down. Inside, he crouched. The cement floor felt gritty and cool beneath his hands. As the boy waited there for his eyes to adjust in the dim light, he pulled from a back pocket his paper lunch sack. He unfolded it. The sack's bright design—racing cars and checkered flags—embarrassed him on the bus and at school. His mother had no idea what a twelve-year-old should carry. Carefully, he formed the opening of the sack in his hand. He brought it to his mouth and blew, inflating the thing. The vague scents of peanut butter, banana, and cut apple surrounded him.

On a nearby shelf, right where he'd first found it, where he'd left it, a long-necked bottle of carburetor cleaner stood soldier proud. The boy took it down. He crossed to the far side of the garage carrying the sack in one hand, shaking the bottle with the other. It felt nearly empty now. He'd worry about that another day, he thought, as he settled onto stacked patio cushions. A shaft of dusty light slanted through the window and across his legs. Robert unscrewed the bottle's tiny black cap. He lifted it to his nose and sniffed. Behind his eyes, something solid seemed to melt.

He could stop right there. The boy was certain of that, certain beyond doubt. He could lean back, rest his head on the rough textured wall, close his eyes, and think multiplication tables. He could recite books of the Bible or state capitals instead. He knew that he wouldn't though. That wasn't why he was here. What did it matter anyway, what happened or didn't happen here in this dark garage, what he did or didn't do? Besides, promises always count as promises, don't they, even those you make to yourself.

Robert pulled the tampon from his pocket. He stripped off the paper wrapping and, with unsteady fingers, fluffed the thing out. He poked and stuffed it down the neck of the bottle until only the string showed. He shook the bottle then, turned it over, and shook it until the sloshing stopped. Then he pulled the soaked tampon out and dropped the thing, still dripping, into the sack.

With jittery hands, Robert shaped the sack's opening. He bent forward, breathed out, breathed hard, and when his lungs felt empty of air, he brought the sack up to cover his nose and mouth. He breathed in, collapsing the sack, drawing fumes into the deep recesses of his lungs. The petroleum fumes, harsh in his throat, bloomed like mainlined sunshine farther down. The earth spun free beneath him. Ancient gravity vanished like some forgotten dream. He felt immaculate, bathed in bright blue crystalline light. His feet buzzed numb, his hands and cheeks too.

The boy inhaled from the sack again. In an ocean surf rush, the world faded away.

Sometime later Robert found himself curled on the cushions. Light through the window glared now. The bright sack drifted beyond his reach, floated out there, and this seemed weirdly funny to the boy. He belched, and the taste of tinny acid came into his mouth. A muffled sensation—something like pain but not really that—throbbed in his head. Robert rolled over. He thought he heard his own distant laugh.

On his hands and knees now, the boy coughed and crawled toward the retreating sack.

At quitting time, Lynette Cole shut down her solder machine. With a thin cedar paddle she skimmed dross from the heated tank.

Lynette had always thought of herself as a fast learner. In her six short months at Gideon Mountain Opportunity Electronics she had mastered wave soldering. She knew her way around the equipment and its controls. She understood thermal profiles and how different solders flowed. She knew all this better than anyone else, woman or man, working there. Others watched the same training tapes, but it was Lynette who'd developed a knack, an understanding of the wave. Rarely did inspectors send Lynette's circuit boards back with colored dots or arrow stickers pointing to flaws—solder bridges, cold joints, or meniscus problems. More often than not, Ansel Jacks, her line supervisor, would route complex circuit boards to her machine, and she knew why. He could count on her to do them right. In all her life, Lynette had never felt so accomplished at something, so respected, so proud.

On her clipboard, she filled out her daily productivity log

sheet for Jacks to tabulate. The supervisor, recently separated from his wife, worked long hours, coming to work early and leaving late. That had been half the problem, he'd confided to her, with his marriage. Jacks would schedule extra hours for Lynette too, on weeks when she had trouble making her bills. Naturally, there was talk around the factory floor and whispered gossip in the locker room about Jacks and his favorite solder girl.

After work she and Jacks would sometimes meet secretly for drinks in a quiet back booth at Lucky Threes out on Highway 1839. Things hadn't gotten the least bit romantic between them though, regardless of what people suspected. This was not an affair. At least it wasn't one yet. It could become one though. Lynette knew that. And she wasn't about to fight it when the time was right. For too long, life had shortchanged her in the romance department. And there was certainly something wonderfully earnest, almost fervent, about Ansel Jacks. His kind of righteous energy got to her. It got under her skin in a thrilling kind of way. Sometimes Lynette would wake up at night and imagine being close, being special, to someone like Jacks. Still, she'd remind herself in the cold light of day, getting tangled up with another married man was the last thing she should do. So she lived with the cheated feeling for now. She'd wait for his divorce to come through. It would all work out then.

In that back booth, Ansel Jacks would talk about pressures from management at work. He'd brag about his son, who was a year older than her Robert and whip smart. And after two beers, Jacks would drift into talk about his marriage, lamenting the shambles it had become. Lynette would tell him about Robert, about the boy's father, about moving from Adkins and how hard things were just then—being single, working, and raising a son. She and Jacks shared drinks and cigarettes. She'd study his expressive face and the way his hands moved on his glass, how he fingered his matchbook as he talked, pinwheeling it mindlessly with those long fingers. Sometimes she'd catch him watching her too, those rich brown eyes studying her. That was it though, the extent of things. It was better than nothing, she'd decided, this way of being with him, but separated by a booth table. And if real romance had to wait, so be it. No one could stop her from imagining in the night what the future might bring.

In the women's locker room, Lynette hung her flux-spattered smock on a locker hook and tossed her disposable hair bonnet at the corner basket. She elbowed her way between others at the long wall mirror to fix her lipstick. She ran a comb through her hair too, for all the good it would do.

There was a flux spot on the midriff of her favorite white blouse. She swore and swiped at it with a damp paper towel. None of the others seemed to notice or care. Most wore old blouses or T-shirts with ancient stains. They complained about weather instead, about gas prices, about unfair workloads, achy joints, and unruly hair. It was the kind of talk that would bring her down if she let it. She didn't though. Lynette believed in the enduring power of hopeful thoughts and bright anticipations. True, things in life didn't usually measure up to her dreams. Disappointment was a constant risk. But she'd learned to shed those feelings immediately, to get up off her pity pot, to find some new reason to hope. Let bad shit build up, she knew, and it would drag you down.

Back at her locker, she changed from her work shoes and straightened the tuck of her blouse into her jeans. She grabbed her cigarette pack and helmet and hurried out to the parking lot. Her Harley waited there.

Lynette looked good on a motorcycle. Her ass looked good on a motorcycle. She'd heard that said enough to know it was true. Robert's father had been the first to tell her so. In fact, he was the one who'd first coaxed her onto a bike and taught her to ride. That was fourteen years ago. She'd been so young, a kid just out of school. She had taken everything for granted back then, all her grand expectations of what the future held.

It still looked good, though, her ass on that motorcycle. That knowledge was a kind of power. Men stared as she sped by. In her mirrors, she'd see them. Over the engine's roar, she'd hear their whoops, their two-fingered whistles, their raunchy calls. She'd gun the engine and, tugging on the handlebars, bring that ass up off the seat and give it a shake as she zigzagged the bike across the centerline of the road, an answering salute to them.

This wasn't a show she'd put on for Jacks. She wouldn't do it when Robert was around either. Or her brother, Jerry, for that matter. Around them, Lynette stayed tame. This was not how a boy should see his mother, after all, not how a brother, no matter how wayward, should see his kid sister. Here and now, though, after a long day at work, on her bike speeding away from town and headed home, Lynette could be this wild woman, or any other woman she might take a mind to be.

The sound of drilling filled Robert's skull. It rattled like a can of marbles.

A deep purple darkness filled the garage. The air felt like wet canvas on his skin. The boy imagined that he might be Jonah deep in the whale's belly. He rolled to his side and, eyes closed again, let himself drift.

The drilling stopped.

Several seconds passed, and then the silence that had arrived so suddenly was replaced by a new noise—a muted metal clattering.

"Fuck," Robert muttered. The word hurt his head. He clamped his hands to his temples to keep his head together. From outside came a muted thud. Someone laughed. The boy got to his knees, looked up at the window and the bright twilight sky outside. Hushed voices—two men, maybe more—voices overlapping each other. Under it all, those dull metal sounds. Then the whirring drill again.

The boy scrambled across to the open window, squatting there against the log wall, looking up at the broad sill. *Shit! How late is it?*

The sounds of drilling and the voices, Robert could tell now, came from somewhere behind the house. He peered over the sill. It was late, too early for stars, but the sun fully down. And still the sky seemed strangely bright and painful to see. He stood, rubbing his eyes. Looking at a slant through the window, he could see most of a small pickup truck at the corner of the house. Robert recognized the primed fender rust-outs, the dangling chrome strip, the sun-crazed paint. It was Jerry Cole's rusty GMC pickup. Nearby, a squat man in a ball cap—not Jerry, Robert was certain of that—hefted a length of copper gutter over the side and dropped it into the truck bed. Did Jerry know, he wondered, how this guy was using his truck?

A small panic took hold of the boy. He tried the door leading into the house. It was locked. He groped at the overhead door until he found the latch handle. If he could lift it and slide out on his belly, he could slip away. No one would ever know he'd been here. But no matter what he twisted, turned, or pulled, the latch mechanism held tight.

With a muffled groan, Robert sank back to the cold cement floor. He sat there, his throbbing forehead against pulled-up knees, and he thought again of the callow boy in the mirror. "Stupid, stupid, stupid," he whispered, rocking. "So fucking stupid."

At first Lynette hadn't worried when she'd come home and found Robert gone. In fact, she was quietly pleased. Her son spent too much time inside for a growing boy, too much time in his room, too much time alone. She didn't remember being like that, not ever in her life. Robert hadn't left a note on the kitchen table, which he sometimes did. He hadn't fed Marty either—it was one of his chores, a lesson in taking responsibility. He must have refilled the dog's water bowl though. It was almost half full.

The greyhound barked now. Lynette went out.

She hoped that Robert had gone off somewhere with one of his friends, some kid who had newer video games maybe or a working satellite dish. If asked, she wouldn't have been able to name who her son's friends might be, not with any certainty. In fact, Lynette had only the vaguest sense of them—except for the Jacks boy, of course. The rest were just names to her, names from school, names he'd mention at dinner when she prodded him to talk about friends.

She started for the back porch and the bag of dog food there. No, she told herself. This was Robert's chore, his responsibility. It was time the boy started learning what life had showed her, what it was still teaching Jerry in even harder ways. Righteous intentions don't count for shit. Someday there'd be no one around to set things right. Deeds matter. Fate trumps faith.

Back in the kitchen, she twisted the cap from a cold beer and drank. She savored the foam in her mouth, the liquid going down. It tasted good. Tasted damn good. Deserved. She carried the bottle with her to the bathroom, stripping off her blouse as she went. At the sink, she soaked the blouse, submerging it, pushing it under the bleach water. Her hands had rosin flux stains, deep and gritty in her knuckle creases, beneath her nails and cuticles. It was the ugly evidence of her work. She'd been ashamed when Jacks first remarked about them at Lucky Threes. "They're stained," she'd told him. "That's all."

What she did after work at the sink felt like a ritual cleansing of fabric and self. As she scrubbed at the sink, it occurred to Lynette that she had never actually met Robert's friends. She'd developed a sense of them, though, from things he'd said. They'd never once come here to see him. She blamed it on their living so far from town, and the guilt of that bothered her. Did her son, she wondered, ever invite them out here? It had been nearly two years since she and Robert moved from Adkins. It didn't seem right that they were still strangers here.

True, their place wasn't very fancy. It wasn't one of those new ditto homes in town or a mansion in the woods. The place was clean though. No one could say otherwise. They had the best well water anywhere, and there wasn't a better view hereabouts unless you hiked up to the west crest of Ponder Ridge. No, Robert had no reason to be ashamed. No reason at all. Shame was the last thing Lynette wanted her son to feel.

She drained the bleach water and ran cold water to rinse the blouse. Then she wrung the fabric and draped it over the shower rod. She neatened it there, buttoned it, and smoothed wrinkles until everything hung straight. In the bedroom, she took a T-shirt from the clothes basket beside the bed. It was her favorite, a black T-shirt, its emblem faded, a concert souvenir from her Brooks and Dunn days. Ansel Jacks liked it. He'd told her so. He called it her boot-scootin' shirt.

Or maybe, it occurred to Lynette as she pulled the shirt on, her son *had* invited school friends here and they'd made excuses. She could believe that. Insecure people often didn't know their own weaknesses. Jealousy, for example. Children picked that up from their parents. That could explain Robert's problem making friends here. In fact, the more Lynette considered this, the more likely the explanation seemed.

In the kitchen, she took two large pizzas from the freezer and set the oven to preheat. Now that Jerry lived with them, he chipped in with grocery money, even though things weren't easy for him right now. His prison record—he'd been caught reselling prescription meds, hardly a major crime—closed too many doors when he looked for work.

Lynette drank from her beer. The bleach smell was still on her hands. It was a clean scent, quick and tight and high in her nose, not at all like the solder flux vapors with their vaguely vomitlike smell that permeated her workplace, nothing like the molten metal fumes that sometimes escaped the vent hood, their taste like new dental fillings in her mouth.

The dog barked again. It seemed such a plaintive sound, and it sent the first worried shudder snaking up Lynette's back.

Robert had been thinking about eagles and hawks, the way soaring birds would just hang in the air—vultures too—when the garage lock snapped open, a ceiling light came on, and the overhead door started up its track. The motor hummed and gears whirred under the strain. The boy gasped, and he scrambled toward cardboard boxes stacked against the far wall.

A chunky, stooped-over man came under the lifting door, a control of some sort in his hand. He straightened and blinked in the light. "What? Who's that?" he said, seeing the boy. He took a couple of quick steps as if to duck back out, then stopped. His arm came up like a rifle pointing at Robert. Overhead, the door motor clicked off. It sounded like a rifle cocking.

The box stack Robert ducked behind was too short to hide him.

"You!" the man yelled. "You stay right there." He kept his hand and the control aimed at Robert as if pinning him there as he worked his way to the side of the garage.

Slowly, the boy stood, his heart racing. "I was sleeping," he said in a hoarse voice. "That's all." His eyes went to the paper sack, so blatant in the middle of the floor. "I have to get home."

"Come here," the man called over his shoulder, yelling to someone out back. He leaned around the corner. "Hey!" he barked. "Climb down and get in here. We got us a trespasser."

A thought like inspiration flashed through Robert's mind. This might be a dream. It might be his brain getting weird on him like it had on jimsonweed. He'd imagined that time that he was at Darlington, watching his secret father—his real one. Robert and his mother were in the grandstand like everyone else, and they heard his father's voice over the public address system calling Robert down. He told the crowd that he needed his son's help on his pit crew. Robert felt his mother's hand on his back, urging him to go, and he felt such incredible joy. In truth, his father had been dead for nearly five years by then, and he had never once raced at big tracks like Darlington. He'd driven fendered cars on short tracks and local dirt tracks. That's all he'd ever been, a weekend racer. The boy knew all this even then, knew it perfectly well in his messed-up brain. Still, the joy had felt real, and so for a short while the boy had let himself believe that his father was alive again. He let himself believe that everything he imagined was real.

The misshapen man at the garage door, Robert realized almost immediately, was not a wild weed dream like before. None of this, not one bit, was what he would wish. The boy turned toward the garage window, and he saw Jerry's face squinting in. Robert felt a sinking inside, like something was falling away.

Jerry came around to the open door. "Jeez, Ketch, kill the damn light." He shoved the squat man aside. His eyes searched the wall for a switch.

"Over there," Robert said, pointing erratically.

Jerry stopped short. "Shit," he said. "It's Lynette's kid."

Ketch looked back at Jerry. "You said this place was abandoned."

"It is abandoned," Jerry said. "Has been for weeks. He don't belong here."

"He's right," the boy said. "I don't."

Jerry seemed to consider things for a minute. "Give me your keys," he told Ketch. "I'll take the kid home."

The boy tried to stumble forward and almost went down. Jerry hurried over and caught him under the arm. He stooped and picked up Robert's lunch sack, the bottom stained and soaked, and he started to lead the boy out. As he did, the overhead light timed out and switched off.

Outside, Ketch punched buttons on the control and the door came down. "You're coming back, right?" he said to Jerry.

"Ten minutes, maybe fifteen. You finish loading the truck."

Jerry helped the boy to the front seat of Ketch's Subaru. "You got gum?" he asked, going around to the driver's side. "Got breath mints, anything like that?"

Robert tried to make sense of the question. There was a stink in the car like sour milk, and he thought that Jerry might mean that. "In my locker at school," the boy said, his voice still raspy from the fumes.

"We'll drive into town for some before I take you home," Jerry said. He set the sack on the console between them and adjusted the driver's seat. "Your breath smells like a goddamn carburetor." He turned the ignition key. The engine coughed and started.

Robert bounced the back of his head against the headrest, the pain there dull and deserved.

Jerry picked up the sack again. He sniffed the bottom and grimaced. He did not look inside. Instead, he handed it across to Robert. The boy took it and held it in his hands like some alien thing. Tears were in his eyes, and an anger at something he could not name came loose in his chest. He crumpled the sack and wadded it into a tight ball. As soon as the car was out on the road, he rolled the window down and tossed the thing out.

The drive into town took forever. The pain inside Robert's skull slowly faded. He rested the side of his head on the cool window and watched lights fly by. With his tongue, he probed the corner of his lip, the sting of a blister there. Gradually the swirl of confused thoughts slowed. Jerry had his window down now, his elbow outside, a toothpick wedged between his teeth.

"You're stupid," he said finally, "sniffing that shit."

"I know," Robert muttered.

"Stupid," Jerry said, louder this time. He took the toothpick out and pointed with it. "And for what?"

The boy shrugged.

"Your mother don't need that crap from you." When Robert didn't answer, Jerry looked over, gave him a shove on the shoulder. "Does she?"

"I know," the boy said, louder this time. With a fingernail he picked at a rip in the armrest. "Every time I do it, I never want to do it again."

"So don't," Jerry said, as if his was the final word. "That's your key right there. Just don't." He pulled into the gravel lot beside Gilly's Gas-N-Go and parked there.

As soon as they were inside, Jerry went straight to the cash register and the girl working there. He started talking in the sweet voice he used around women. Holly, he called her. The coloring of her skin, uniform and slightly orange, indicated regular sessions in tanning beds. Her face was slender, her eyes quite small but alive now as Jerry leaned across the counter and talked to her. To Robert, their conversation seemed secretive yet somehow familiar, intimate even, in ways he could not comprehend.

The boy picked out a packet of green Tic Tac mints and a jug of red Gatorade from the cooler along the back wall. As he brought them to the cash register, Holly was pointing at the door. "There's a phone on the side of the building," she said. "You know there is. That's what you're supposed to use."

"It's a local call, honey," he said. "It won't cost Gilly nothing."

Holly looked down the snacks aisle and out to the pumps, where a man was putting gas in his SUV. "I shouldn't," she said. Her voice was almost a whisper. "Really, I shouldn't," she said again. Even as she said it, she reached under the counter and brought out a beige telephone. With a moment of hesitation and then a shy smile, she slid it across to Jerry. He took it and punched numbers.

"That wasn't too hard, now was it?" he said.

The girl grabbed Robert's drink and mints to scan. "Ain't nothing about you too hard for me," the girl said. She didn't look up from her scanning and bagging.

"Lynette?" Jerry said into the phone. He grabbed a large Kit Kat bar from beside his elbow and slid it down the counter to the boy, motioning to ring it up too.

"The boy's fine, Sis," Jerry said. "He's with me." He listened. He winked at Robert and worked his jaw so his toothpick twitched. "He's okay," he said. "Just calm down."

Robert paid Holly and pocketed the change. She fluffed open a bag, but before she could put the Kit Kat in, Jerry grabbed it away and ripped into the package with his teeth. "He's helping me work on Ketch's car," he said. "Yes, now. You remember Ketch." Jerry waggled his head and made a mocking face for Robert and the girl to see. "Another hour, I'd guess."

Jerry listened, chewing. "Didn't I just tell you, Sis?" he said.

"Didn't I just tell you the boy's all right? He's fine. Take your chill pill. Take two."

Robert knew all about his mother's chill pills, that prescription bottle bearing a stranger's name that she kept hidden on the medicine cabinet's top shelf. He'd even counted them to know when she took one. Once daily as needed, the label read. Needed. Sometimes the boy wondered about his own need, wondered how it measured up. More than once he'd thought he might try one, or maybe a half. But then it had occurred to him that his mother might keep count too.

"Cold pizza is good," Jerry said. "It's fine. Okay . . . right . . . good-bye." He hung up hard and pushed the phone away. "You got five dollars?" he asked Robert, and when the boy said he did, Jerry told the girl, "Tear us off five of them scratch tickets, darling."

Lynette had phoned Ansel Jacks in a moment of weakness. It wasn't like Robert to simply disappear, after all. She must have seemed totally flustered to Jacks, phoning like that, almost begging him to drive out. For what? What had life ever dished out that she couldn't handle? She was not a woman who panics. That was simply not her way. And then, not ten minutes later, Jerry had called and said that Robert was with him. Of course she'd called Jacks back immediately. All she got by then, though, was his answering machine.

Why hadn't she just poured herself a tall glass of Jack Daniels instead or mixed a pitcher of margaritas? Or maybe she should have taken one or two of those pills, like Jerry said, and ridden the evening out.

Lynette checked her watch. Jacks could pull up any minute now. She shoved the pizzas back into the still-warm oven. Then she made a quick run through the house, straightening couch pillows, stacking newspapers, and closing bedroom doors.

Marty barked, and she looked out to see her boss's silver Camry stop out front. Ansel Jacks climbed out and came toward the house. In creased jeans, pearl-buttoned western shirt with the cuffs rolled up, and bright white sneakers, he looked downright hand-some, like a clothes model sprung to life.

She opened the door. "Robert's okay," she said, coming out. "I was stupid, worrying, calling you like that. He's with my brother."

Jacks stopped at the steps.

"They're working on a car," she said. "It was so stupid of me," she said again, "calling you like that." Bugs swarmed the porch light beside her, pinging themselves against the bulb.

"It's okay," he said. "Worrying is what mothers do. If only Zach's mother worried more." With one white sneaker on the first step, he leaned forward, one hand on his bent knee and the other deep in a pocket, like a catalog pose.

"They'll be home in a while," she heard herself say. "Less than an hour."

Jacks looked left and right. "I like your place," he said, and he came up the steps. She stepped aside, moved closer to the light. With a hand on the doorjamb, he peered through the screen. "Nice," he said.

"I'm really sorry about this, Ansel," she said softly. His name felt intimate on her lips.

Jacks reached into his shirt pocket. The hand came out empty. "In all that rush," he said, still patting the pocket, "I forgot my cigarettes."

She opened the screen door and stepped inside, and he was there beside her. "It's not much," Lynette said. She made a sweeping gesture around the room and then turned to go for the cigarettes.

His hand was on her shoulder, stopping her, and she didn't pull away. "Lynette," he said, "it's perfect." He pulled her to him, and she let him. His arms went around her, one hand tangled in her hair, the other low on her back, and she was tight against him, feel-ing the length of him against her, the urgency in his breathing, and the beating of his heart in her ear.

She looked up and kissed him then, a gentle kiss, a child's kiss, and his hand worked its way up under her T-shirt and bra and onto her breast, and Jacks kissed her harder then, all tongue and teeth, and she nipped at his lip and her hands popped open the snaps of his shirt.

In the car outside Gilly's Gas-N-Go, Jerry held a lottery scratch card against the steering wheel and scratched with his lucky dime. Robert popped a second breath mint into his mouth and then a third. "Was she worried about me," he asked, "on the phone?"

Jerry ripped the ticket both ways and scattered the pieces out the window. "Worry is all she knows how to do."

"I'm better now." The boy cupped a hand over his mouth and nose to check his breath. "I should get home." When Jerry didn't say anything, the boy added, "I didn't feed the dog."

Jerry gave a small laugh. "You don't care nothing about that dog. What a waste of good money, me buying a greyhound for you and then gathering up all the makings for a pen and even hauling them."

"I like him," Robert said. "I like him fine." Saying the words, the boy could hear the lie in them, and it saddened him.

Jerry punched the boy's shoulder, punched it hard. "I was just funning you," he said. "The people that moved from that fancy log house give him to me. Marty didn't cost me a nickel."

Robert's shoulder throbbed, and so did something low in his gut. Maybe he was feeling sad and sorry for himself, but there was no way he'd let himself start crying. "Why'd you say it then?" he asked.

"It's a joke, son. Your ma's right. You've got to toughen up, learn to take jokes," Jerry said.

Robert had little idea how to be tough or make himself tough, and he knew it. He wasn't even sure it was something he wanted to be. And even if he did get tough someday, he doubted that he'd ever see anything funny in Jerry's kinds of jokes.

"Besides, son," Jerry said, scratching the dime across another lottery card, "we can't go home yet. Your mouth might taste better, but you still got them fumes all down in your lungs. Your ma thinks we been working on a car, but still . . ." He ripped the card and tossed the pieces. "There's better ways than huffing, you know," he said, "not so obvious."

Robert did know. In the back of the school bus, Zach Jacks would sometimes spike his friends' Gatorades, their Mountain Dew jugs and sport drinks, adding a little vodka for those who wanted, something to get them through the day. The bus driver, the teachers, no one could tell. That was the great thing about vodka, how people could hardly smell it on someone. More than once, Robert had tried to come up with a way to get his hands on a bottle. Then he could offer to spike drinks on the bus the way Zach Jacks did.

"Yow!" Jerry pounded the steering wheel with his hand. "Yee-ow and hot damn!" He held up the scratch-off for the boy to see. "Eighty bucks, boy!" he exclaimed. Robert took the ticket and held it at an angle near the windshield. "Didn't I tell you this dime's lucky? Ain't that what I said not five minutes ago?"

Robert couldn't take his eyes off the card, the numbers there. He felt a strange thrill, a kind of joy, inside. "Lucky," he said. "That's exactly what you said."

Jerry hurriedly scratched the last card and blew the scrapings away. He studied the numbers for a second as if not believing them. Then he handed the ticket to the boy and took the other ticket back. "That one's yours, son. This one's mine."

Robert checked it, but none of the numbers matched. "A loser?" he said.

"Most are," Jerry said. He looked at the winning ticket again as if wanting to be sure. "You know what, kid?" He said. "Let's go somewhere and celebrate. What do you say? You and me. A whorehouse maybe. Or Holly's place later. She's always up for a party."

Robert studied the dashboard. He could feel his face redden.

"Relax," Jerry said. "Jeez, kid. I'm kidding about the whorehouse. You shoulda seen your face!"

"Just go cash the ticket, okay?" the boy said. "We'll split the money, and you can take me home."

"Split it? It's my ticket, son, my lucky dime," Jerry said, leaning closer. "Don't you forget who it was I found huffing bad shit tonight."

"My money bought those tickets," Robert said. He clamped his hands between his knees. "Besides," he said, "if I'm in trouble, you're in more. I seen you and Ketch thieving copper."

Jerry glanced at the boy and then looked away. "Son," he said, throwing an arm over the seatback, "let me explain this to you so you'll understand. That log house was a guaranteed sitting duck for real copper thieves, those gutters an open invitation. They see a house like that and they'll do more than take down gutters. They'll bust out walls to get at pipes and wiring. That's how they do. Ketch and me, we just might be saving the place from all that."

Robert flapped the losing ticket against his pant leg. He didn't dare look over. "You think Lem Tate sees things that way?" His head was feeling clearer now.

Jerry grabbed the back of the boy's neck and forced his face down to his knees. "You little shit," he said. "I'm trying to tell you, friendly-like, how things are."

A jolt of pain shot through Robert's body, and he tried to break free.

"You say anything to Sheriff Tate," Jerry whispered near his ear, "say one word, and I will seriously mess you up. You got that?" He gave Robert's neck one final shove and then let go.

The boy wiped his nose on a sleeve. "Just take me home," he said. "Your buddy Ketch must be done and waiting by now. Or maybe he's lit out with the load."

"Here's another lesson for you, son." From his pocket, Jerry took the pickup keys and jangled them high in the air. "Don't trust no one you can't watch. Got it?"

Robert nodded.

Jerry opened the car door, got out, and then poked his head back through the window. "I'm going inside to cash this ticket," he said. "Then I'm taking you home. And you won't say nothing about nothing to your ma or anyone else. Are we clear about that?"

"I bought the tickets," Robert said. "It's not fair."

Jerry said, "I'll give you your five dollars back. Can't nothing be fairer than that, now can it?"

The boy couldn't make himself answer.

"That prize can't be yours, Robby boy, not legally. Read that ticket you're holding," Jerry said, pointing. "Turn it over and read. You got to be eighteen to win."

A new anger rose, warm and wet, in the boy's tight throat.

The man shoved away from the car. "You don't look no eighteen to me, son," Jerry said. He turned, his work boots scrunching gravel, and he went back inside to claim his prize.

He wasn't gone long—three minutes, maybe four—and he came out happy, the cash all fanned out and flapping for Robert to see. But those three or four minutes had been time enough for the boy to drop coins in the pay phone at the side of the building, time enough to tell the 911 dispatcher in his still-raspy voice that a suspicious GMC pickup was parked behind the vacant log mansion off Route 1095, time enough to hang up and get back into the passenger seat of Ketch's smelly Subaru.

It wasn't at all romantic, Lynette's long-imagined first time with Ansel Jacks. It was nothing like she'd expected. Everything was rushed and awkward on their way to the bed and then interrupted by her frantic search through drawers for a condom. All the while Marty had barked outside as if Jerry and Robert might have just driven up, as if they might be parking out front at that very moment.

And when it was over, a terrible silence existed between her and Jacks. They rolled from bed and retrieved clothes and dressed, all the while hardly seeming to notice each other in the dimly lit room. Lynette took her disappointment to the kitchen. She got out the bottle of J. D. and poured a glass over ice for herself and another for him. He came into the kitchen, snapping the cuffs of his shirt, tucked the shirttail, and took the glass from her hand.

Jacks raised his drink as if toasting her and sipped. "Maybe I can have that cigarette now?" he said.

She tapped one from the pack for him and another for herself. She lit both and handed one to him. He took it and thanked her, and they smoked in silence and drank.

"You should go," Lynette said at last. "Robert will be home any time now, and Jerry. I'm not ready to explain you yet."

In that moment she saw his surprise, an expression so brief but unmistakable on his face, one unguarded moment before Jacks gathered himself and smiled too broadly. "Right," he said.

It bothered her, walking out with him, and she knew she should let it go, knew she should shut up and let this evening end now, end in just this ungainly way, if she ever wanted some kind of future with Jacks. She managed, in fact, to stifle herself until they got out to his car, until he reached out to kiss her again.

"You didn't believe me," she said, and she felt her heart sink at the sound of her own voice. "When I called you all panicky about Robert," she said, "you thought I made that up?"

Jacks shrugged. "I believed you," he said, "more or less." He dropped his cigarette and mashed it under a sneaker that seemed too white in the evening moonlight. "But when I get out here, there's no emergency. I'm no fool. I see what's happening, or think I do, and I'm totally up for it." He reached for Lynette, but she backed away.

"You should go," she said, "before they get back." There was a stone in the bottom of her stomach the size of his fist.

He hesitated, as if searching for words to say, and then opened the car door.

As she turned to go back inside, she saw one side of the rusty wire pen bent down. She went over to look.

"What is it?" Jacks called over to her.

"The dog's loose again. He keeps going back to his old home," she said, pointing, "this place through the woods." She turned back to the pen, as if to convince herself that Marty was really gone. Near the top of the bent wire, a small patch of gray fur was snagged. "Shit," she said, reaching for the patch. It was sticky with blood.

"What is it?" Jacks called again.

"He hung a leg in the fence wire."

Lynette hurried inside for a flashlight. As she came back down off the porch, she saw Jacks near the pen. He had a battery lantern in his hand, and he swept its beam across the ground. "He's bleeding some," he said.

"You go," Lynette said, waving him away. "I can handle this."

A confused look crossed his face. "Let me—" he said, something like frustration erupting. He switched off the lantern with an angry poke and headed back to his car.

She went into the woods, following her weak beam down the path. Every few yards she'd see traces of Marty's blood, small spots on the ground, and she knew for certain where he was headed. Several times she stopped to call the dog's name and to listen in the still night air. As she neared the bottom, she could hear water ripple in the creek and then skidding footfalls behind her. She turned to see Ansel Jacks, his bright sneakers and lantern beam coming down the path.

She felt her anger at the man rise again, although she wasn't sure why. "I don't need your help," she said as he came near.

"Got it," Jacks said, his hands up in surrender. "No help needed."

"That's right." She started across the stream, stepping on the first rock, leaping to the second and the third. She stopped there, shining her light near her feet and on the last rock. There were no blood spots, no wet places either, where Marty had crossed. In her chest, Lynette's heart thumped like a log drum.

"Just tagging along." His singsong voice sounded close behind her. "Your batteries could run down, you know. You'd be stuck out here, a woman alone in the dark. Or you might need someone strong to carry the dog. You'll be glad I'm here then."

She wanted to tell him to shut up, just follow her if that's what he wanted to do. Quit being a jerk about it, for God's sake, she'd tell him, if she had the nerve.

Lynette imagined the injured greyhound somewhere up ahead,

struggling up the hill on that damaged leg. Or maybe he'd strayed off the path, was tangled somewhere and bleeding. Sick pets sometimes went away to hide and die. How often had she heard that? She couldn't bear the thought of Marty doing that, couldn't live with that image in her head.

Halfway up, she stopped and called the dog's name, and then she heard a thrashing ahead in the brush. It came from up the trail to her left. Jacks, farther back, shined his lantern in that direction. She called again and listened. "He must be out now," she said, a thrill running through her, "or nearly out. There's an open field up there and a huge yard." She waited for Jacks to catch up and, when he did, reached back and took his hand.

They climbed again, both breathless now. Ahead, Lynette could see the tops of two giant wind turbines against the clear night sky. Then a third one appeared, the three of them standing apart, their bases hidden still by the crest of the hill. Flashes of red and blue reflected from the slender metal blades, the colors strobing like bright carnival lights.

Singing Second Part

The afternoon Eddie Kenton gunned the engine on his new '67 Mustang outside the Embry house, I expect he thought I'd come running out all moony-eyed and giggly. He was twenty. I'd just turned fifteen, although folks generally take me for older. Most girls considered Eddie handsome, and he seemed to share that opinion. Didn't matter to me. Katy Davies had more important concerns than showy boys with fast cars.

Maybe he thought he was first to come around. He wasn't, and not by a long shot. He was just first here in Spivey. Back when I lived home, Reverend McVey's boy Wallace, who's ever bit as good-looking and a whole lot more savvy, came calling. He lived over the ridge from us. The Burridge twins showed interest too. If I'd stayed longer in Little Piney, I expect Wallace and the twins would have had it out. I'll never know, because before anything could get to brewing, President Johnson spoke to my daddy, and he sent me here to live with his aunt's second cousin, Ruth Etta Embry, and her husband, Raymond.

Ruth Etta is a fleshy woman given to blue fits. That's why her husband took me in, even though I was one more mouth to feed. He needed someone reliable to cook and help out with housework and children whenever Ruth Etta felt poorly, which was most all the time since her newest baby was born. Being oldest back home, I knew my way around a kitchen and a crib. At one time or another I bottle-nursed and diapered ever last one of my brothers and sisters except Marilyn, who's only two years younger than me. Which is to say that helping out Ruth Etta wasn't that much new for me. Never once did I feel like I was freeloading off Raymond Embry's table, although to hear him tell, you'd think that I was doing nothing to pull my weight, that I was snatching food right out of his own children's mouths. Luckily, before sending me off, Daddy cautioned me on how Embrys are. So I've tried hard to not take Raymond's ways personal.

The main problem with Eddie's revving the Mustang's engine out front that particular Sunday afternoon was that Ruth Etta was feeling especially poorly. She'd even skipped church service that morning, and, in penance, she'd stretched herself out on the parlor couch and was listening to radio ministries. I'd got the baby and the two-year-old down for naps, so I slipped out and tried to shush Eddie.

The boy made like he didn't see me coming. He started flicking one of his dashboard gages like it's stuck, which I'm sure it wasn't. When I got to the curb, he gave the dash a *whoomp* with the heel of his hand and said, "There," acting all satisfied like he'd fixed something. Back home, I drove truck enough to know that slamming a dash won't likely do much good.

"Can you please shut that off?" I asked as polite as I know how.

He gunned it twice more, then let it die back to an idle.

"Timings still not quite right," he said.

"Sounded fine to me," I said.

"She's set six before top dead center." He puffed his cigarette and tried to blow a smoke ring. The wind tore it up. "Manual says four, but she runs better set at six."

"Mrs. Embry isn't feeling well today, Eddie. I'd appreciate you keep the noise down."

"Engine like this is made to run loud." He thumped his palm on the outside of the door. "Get in. We'll go for a spin."

"I've got chores." Besides which, I had important plans for my future—plans that did not include Sunday cruising with a citified Romeo. I planned on going to college one day. First in our family, near as Daddy and I could figure. And me a girl to boot.

"I got gas to burn," he said. "Just a run out to the interstate and back. They won't even know you're gone."

"I can't, Eddie. Really."

He gunned the engine and popped the clutch. The tires squealed, and the car lurched forward a few feet. Then he grinned and did it again.

"Eddie! I asked you keep it quiet."

"And I asked you come ride with me."

The boy is nothing but irritation.

"All right," I said. "But you got to Bible-swear you'll never ever come driving by their house again."

"Let's go," he said.

We didn't just run out to the interstate and back. We went there, but then Eddie drove through the center of Spivey, which, thank God, was mostly deserted, and then out to the railroad overpass. He played the radio low and carried on about his older brother, G.W., who was just back in town after graduating college. Eddie wanted no part of that. He'd learned a good trade—carpentering—straight out of high school. His father, who built houses, pulled strings and got him into the union. All the new construction around Somerset kept him busy six days a week. When he could, he worked on furniture, though, making new, fixing old. It was slow work, he said. But running a hand across one new bookcase was better than looking at a street full of framed houses. I envied him his talent—creating beauty with his hands.

He drove slow again through the center of town, then dropped me back at the Embry place. I thanked him for the ride and reminded him about our deal, which he pretended not to remember. But when he drove off, he kept the engine quiet.

In all of this, I did nothing to lead the boy on. Mostly I listened and didn't say much. If he'd had the sense God gave him, he'd know

I was not the least bit interested in him. Which is not to say I couldn't be in a different situation, because the boy does have several admirable aspects.

In my short life, I've seen too many young girls hitched and having babies well before they're full-grown themselves. Momma, rest her soul, was but sixteen when she married Daddy. Grandma Webb was no older than I am now when she and Papaw tied the knot. She always allowed that it was best that way. Maybe so. Then again, there was Momma. One time she told me she wished she'd gone different places and did more things before she settled into family life. She hugged me and said she'd never trade me for nothing, but I'd figured out that I was a six-month baby. I know that I was the reason Momma never got to go and do like she wanted. One thing was sure. I wasn't getting myself tied down young. I was finishing high school, and I was going to be the first of our Davies in college. I'd do it for Daddy and for Momma and for Grandma Webb too. And I'd do it for me. So Eddie Kenton might as well pack up his sweet-talking ways and just go fly hisself a kite.

Back home, fitting in was never a problem for me. Maybe that's because I knew most everyone. Spivey has more folks than a body can possibly know. I'm a talker, which helps. Daddy always said there was no silence I wouldn't jump in and fill.

Before I left Little Piney, Brother McVey, who preaches at True Word Baptist Church, wrote me an introduction letter. He sealed it with green wax and said bring it to the preacher at the Bethel Baptist as soon as I got here. The whole way coming I fretted over what that letter said about me. I especially hoped it didn't mention about our poverty. My second day in town I delivered the writing.

Pastor Hawkes had more teeth than mouth, and he wore them in a forever smile. He turned out to be a big help. He got me joined right in, assigning me my very own Sunday school class—second graders—to teach. I expect that letter said something about shape-note singing, because Pastor Hawkes sent me straight off to the choir director, a doughy-complected, dour-eyed lump of a man named

Mr. Widicus. He said I should sing the third verse of "In the Garden" right there on his stoop, which I did. Then he said to sing it again, this time the second part. Second part has always been easier for me. It's the part I learned from singing with Momma. I didn't tell him that though. I just sang.

He fetched me a choir robe. It was faded to the color of plum jelly gone bad. The robe needed taking up at the hem, but it had plenty of room for growing into. He said practice was Wednesdays at eight in the church building basement and that I owed it to the others to be punctual. I should stand between the altos and sopranos when we sang and always sit with good posture and never chew gum.

At supper that evening, Raymond told me that I'd best stay on the smiley side of Mr. Widicus. Besides directing the Bethel Baptist Church choir, he was president of Farmers First Bank, and he headed both the school board and the county draft board. If I'd known all this before, I'd have messed up for sure.

First practice I wore my robe, which no one else did. No mention was made, and I did appreciate that.

It was two weeks after Eddie Kenton raised that ruckus outside the Embry house that I first noticed him at church. One advantage of singing choir is you can watch people while the preaching goes on. Those in the congregation have to crane themselves all around to know who's there and who's not. If Eddie had been a churchgoer before, I'd have noticed. Then he started hanging around after service, keeping me company while I stacked up hymnals and collected leftover bulletins. He talked about general stuff, nothing special. I've always held a low opinion of girls who lead boys on. So I was cautious around Eddie, never overly sociable. Polite and nothing more.

Pastor Hawkes announced that, come November, there would be a two-day country gospel singing over in Evansville, which is in Indiana. The whole choir was planning to go. I phoned Daddy and asked if he'd permit it, me having never been outside Kentucky before. He said it was for me to decide as long as the Embrys allowed.

Back in the second war, Papaw fought against Hitler. He signed up and went off to Italy, even though he had five children at the time. He went because of the children, he'd joke to me. Daddy never did travel that far. Which is not to say that he hadn't gotten around more than most in Little Piney. Last winter a federal man came by. He chose certain folks from the hills to go down to Memphis and testify as a favor to President Johnson at his poverty hearings. They picked Daddy, so he traveled clear across the state and down into Tennessee and over by the Mississippi River. Everything was paid by the United States government. We considered it an honor, what with the country waging war against the Communists in Viet Nam, that President Johnson still took an interest in plain folks' circumstances. I helped Daddy write a speech where he said so, but someone in Memphis told him that wasn't a wise thing to say.

In Memphis, Daddy said he had his picture took more times in three days than ever in his entire life. He testified about how we lived back in the hills, how blessed we felt, even in trying times. It was there that he learned about our poverty, although it was weeks after his returning before I'd hear first word about it.

We always knew there were folks real poverty-poor. But we believed that the poorest people lived bunched up in big cities, all crammed together and breathing used air with no gardens or trees. We had more room than we could possibly use. Maybe we didn't have ever food we might want just when we wanted it, but it was a rare night that I went to bed wishing for more to eat.

For several weeks after that, I'd seen Daddy pondering something. I didn't prod, just waited until he was ready. Then he told me what he'd heard.

The government said that we lived in poverty, on account of he did not have a good factory job that paid more than so much. They showed a movie of President Johnson speaking to Congress where he condemned "the shameful poverty in our midst." Those were his exact words. Daddy memorized them. He was always a proud man, never shamed before, so this hit him real hard. But he was also a man who did what needed doing, once he righted himself. He was determined that his children would not be second class. He'd been fetching about for a way to get me away from Little Piney and the mountains, which he figured was most of the problem. That's when he came up with the idea to send me off to live with the Embrys. I'll help find someplace for Marilyn next, soon as she's old enough. Daddy says he's too deep-rooted back there to leave, but that shouldn't hold the rest of us back.

So when I telephoned to ask permission for the singing in Evansville, I pretty much knew what he'd say. Asking the Embrys would be another matter.

When I asked Ruth Etta could I go, she said okay but ask Raymond. I told Raymond she said okay and asked would he and Ruth Etta be going too. He skips church more times than he goes, so I figured he'd be disinclined, which he was. But he suggested I find someone to look after the children and take Ruth Etta along, on the notion that religious reviving might do her some good.

She liked the idea right off. From that moment on she talked about nothing but the spirit of God, which she knew for certain would visit everyone. There were several groups from our church planning to go. Pastor Hawkes up and chartered a bus so he could drive his flock himself.

Ruth Etta was all the time slipping me folding money from what Raymond budgeted to her for groceries. More often than not, she'd need it back a day later, on account of she'd forgotten something or run out. Whenever she gave me extra money, I'd thank her sincerely. Then I'd squirrel it away. I figured it wasn't really mine until I'd had it a few days.

When the bus sign-up sheet was hung, I had enough seasoned money. I paid my four dollars and asked Ruth Etta for hers. She said it would never do for her to spend all that time on a bus. The woman is easy embarrassed. She explained that she'd have to stop at least once on the trip to use a restroom. Maybe more. No way would she fit in the one they have on a bus. And she'd be much too mortified to ask Brother Hawkes to stop on account of her with the whole congregation knowing why. No, she said. She'd be needing a car ride.

Ruth Etta held a driver's license, and she owned a black Buick. But she didn't drive highways. I could drive anywhere, but Kentucky wasn't quite ready to license me. Over the next few days, she tried to get Raymond to drive. He took me aside and said I should work out a travel arrangement with the young man with a Mustang, the one he'd seen sniffing around after church. I'd sooner eat dirt and I told him so. That's when Raymond took it upon himself to propose the arrangement directly to Eddie Kenton, who agreed.

That got my back up, and I told Ruth Etta in no uncertain terms that I would not go. She complained to Raymond that she wouldn't feel safe unless I was along. He started threatening to send me packing back to Little Piney if I didn't get Ruth Etta to that singing.

Which is how I came to spend time with the one young man in Spivey who most needed discouraging.

I made Ruth Etta promise she'd keep him occupied. To be safe, I wrote myself out a list of conversation topics and memorized it, against the chance Eddie and I ended up alone and he took to talking moonlight and mush. So by the time the weekend of the singing came around, I had things pretty well in hand.

The ladies in the choir told me that southern gospel singings are considerably different from the shape-note singings I knew back home. These singing groups would be mostly professional. Some even packed along their own piano players. Growing up, I sang the Sacred Harp alongside Momma. No piano, just voices, up to a hundred of them, all singing in old-timey parts. Momma usually took first part, and I took second. Sometimes we swapped. Churches from miles around sent their best to Sacred Harp singings. There'd be all the brought-vittles you could imagine—sweet potato casserole, persimmon pudding, hog meat, and whole tables filled with steaming, ravenous-smelling dishes to fortify us all after we'd sung ourselves empty.

The Bethel Baptist ladies said in Evansville there'd be no dinner on the grounds, and I'd hear new songs and sweet harmonies, which disappointed me because I truly yearned to hear the shape-note sounds. I should also expect, they said, a goodly portion of revival preaching and soulful testifying.

Eddie Kenton arrived outside the Embry house just before seven on Saturday morning. His hair was cut short. The Mustang gleamed with new wax. As we sat in the parlor waiting for Ruth Etta to come down, I caught a whiff of his Old Spice. I excused myself and ran upstairs to retrieve my conversation topics list, which I slipped into my purse.

For weeks I'd worried about me sitting beside Eddie for that long ride. As we stepped off the porch and walked down the sidewalk, I could see that it wouldn't happen that way. The car only had two doors. Whoever sat in back had to squeeze through an opening no wider than a fence with a single picket missing. There was no way Ruth Etta could fit. It had to be me in the back. I expect it dawned on Eddie then, because I swear the boy seemed to deflate.

We joined up with the church bus at the high school and followed it onto the interstate headed north and then west. As expected, we weren't ten miles past Lexington when Ruth Etta called for the first rest stop. That's when we lost the bus and started following the map.

Most of the way she chattered away about singings and symptoms and people from high school who she hadn't seen in forever. Eddie nodded politely, but I could tell he wasn't really listening. I couldn't blame him. Sometimes I forget to listen too.

The singing took place in a church building ten times the size of Little Piney Grade School. The music sounded all right, but it lacked the spiritual feel. I thought maybe the Holy Spirit was passing me by on account of I'd compared this in my mind to back-home singings. So I stopped that.

Some voices were truly grand, and some blends too. Course basses scraped deep bottom, the tenors stretching ear-splitting high. Between songs, one or another of the singers testified about how the Lord had guided and touched their music ministry. Still, the gathering was coming up short on fervor. Folks seemed tight, their butts glued to the pews. More than once, Ruth Etta came to her feet. But then she'd look around, see she was the only one, and would have to sit back down.

The mood changed the minute young Brother Joshua King took the stage. The boy, no older than me, has a voice to shame angels. He strutted, slender and tall, across the stage dressed in bright white, and that included his shoes. His hair looked painted on. Even as he whooped and hopped about, hardly one strand moved.

Folks were up now and out in the aisle as Brother Joshua pranced and sang and testified how Jesus had saved him from all sorts of sin and temptation in his young life. A forest of uplifted arms swayed, reaching hands toward him. He seemed to shine as he glided about, glided like he had wings. Brother Joshua called upon the Lord to stamp out every last vestige of the Devil here in the United States, and while He was about it, to strike down the cowardly Viet Cong warring against our brave American boys. Then he recounted his own struggles against the demons of the Evil One, reenacting the trembling fits that possessed his young body during those titanic battles. He sang of the beauty of the heaven God had permitted his humble servant to glimpse. Then he called upon the healing powers of his Lord and Master to move among the faithful gathered here today and, if it be His will, to heal those afflicted by miseries of this world. After one quick mention of the voluntary offering box located to the rear, he finished up with a singing of "In the Garden," which brought back memories of Momma and left me snuffling back tears.

Eddie Kenton sat three rows ahead with Mary Kale's dragged-along husband. At some point, Mr. Widicus had squeezed in beside him. They seemed less taken by Brother Joshua than the others. In fact, they were ignoring the goings on, disagreeing about something, it seemed. Mr. Widicus jabbed his finger into Eddie's chest. Eddie's face clenched like a fist, but then he seemed to back down. He got up and left by a side door. Remembering what Raymond had said about staying on Mr. Widicus's better side, I hoped Eddie had just slipped out for a smoke.

The stir created by young Brother Joshua King's singing and preaching continued long after he'd finished. I expect that older women dreamed of a son like him. Younger ones wished that some-day he might be their angel, their husband, the father of their children. I did not wish such things of course. But I do know how girls my age can be.

When Ruth Etta returned from the ladies' room, a new quartet was working some fine harmony. The gathering hadn't settled down, and neither had she. She carried on about the angel-boy and his message, testifying vehemently to those seated nearby that the Holy Spirit called down upon the gathering by Brother Joshua had mi-raculously lifted her chronic melancholy. I hoped the cure would last long enough for Raymond to see.

The day ended with all the groups onstage and singing. There was a final prayer that tomorrow would bring a revival of old-time religion the likes of which had never before been seen in America. We should all return the next day by one o'clock sharp, and mean-while tell our friends how the Lord was at work in Evansville.

Eddie had the car warmed up when we came out into the cold. His face was somber, and I wondered if it was the message of the day bothering him or something Mr. Widicus had said. On our way to find the motel, Ruth Etta got quiet too. This was strange for her anytime but especially now, considering the miracle visited upon her this afternoon. Her eyes darted about as if she expected some-thing to attack at almost any second.

We found the motel, and Eddie parked out front. Ruth Etta opened her door, worked herself up out of the seat, then shuffled haltingly across to the office. Her gaze swept the pavement every step of the way.

Eddie leaned against the Mustang and zipped his jacket to his neck. He lit a cigarette and offered me one. He knew better, and I told him so. He stuffed his hands into his pockets and said it had turned downright cold. I agreed. He said he enjoyed the singing, which was more polite than true. I knew for fact that he'd rather spend his weekend working on that car or sanding wood. As for me, maybe the Evansville singing was better than most of its kind. But to say it true, I'd take a shape-note singing before that kind any day.

Eddie didn't say anything about Mr. Widicus, and I didn't ask.

I smothered a yawn. I'd sleep well tonight. But first I planned an hour or two watching the color TV at no extra charge, which was promised on a neon sign overhead.

When Ruth Etta came back, her face was flushed and her chin trembled like she was fixing to cry.

"Don't be mad at me now," she said.

"What's the matter?"

"Well . . ." She searched the pavement as she walked around the car and into the grass nearby. "The motel money is gone."

"You were robbed?" I asked.

"Don't you dare tell Raymond."

"Tell me."

"It seemed like the right thing." She turned all liquid.

I grabbed her arm. "What?"

"And don't you dare tell Pastor or anyone," she said.

"Tell what, for heaven's sake."

"I put our motel money in the love offering box at the back of the church." She sounded small and fragile, if you didn't look at her. "It felt like the right thing, like it's what God wanted."

"Thirty-two dollars?" I exclaimed. "You gave it all?"

"Brother Joshua wrought me a miracle. All I had to return was that small sum."

Eddie wandered away, like he was studying a blue Corvette three cars over. More likely he was stifling himself.

"What about our room for tonight?"

"I trusted the Lord would provide, Katy. I truly did."

"You'll have to borrow."

"Oh no! No one can know." She raised her voice so Eddie would hear.

"It's your business," Eddie said, opening his billfold. "Nothing for me to discuss. I've got eight extra."

She looked expectantly to me.

There was no need looking in my purse. I'd set aside five dollars for tomorrow's meals. That was it, and that was what I told her.

For the first few miles of the drive back home, Ruth Etta swung between apologies and threats. If word ever got out, there'd be hell to pay, she said over and over. The day's excitement finally caught up with her as we drove through Corydon. Her head lolled over onto Eddie's shoulder, and her breathing got deep and regular. I felt relieved for her, that she could escape her mortification now. I was relieved for Eddie too. He hadn't asked for this, didn't deserve it, and probably wished he was someplace else. Ruth Etta snorted and curled her considerable self against him.

First flakes of snow float through the headlight beams. They're half-dollar-sized and spaced out at first so you can almost count them. They streak past the windows. They skim across the hood and shoot straight up the windshield, all fluffy like pillow down. The car's speed seems real now, surrounded but hardly touched by glancing flakes of snow.

Eddie hasn't said a word in ever so long. Not that I blame him, considering how the day worked out for him. The least I can do is provide him some company on our long drive home. So I think through my backup conversations list, the one intended for when he turned romantic on me, which clearly is not about to happen. Not tonight.

"You enjoy the singing?" I ask. My voice breaks the warm silence inside. It seems to startle him.

"I wasn't that much in the revival mood," he says.

"You have to be in the mood," I tell him. "That's for sure."

Another minute of silence. Maybe two.

"How old would you take Brother Joshua for?" I ask.

"Sixteen?"

"He seems so intelligent for that age."

Nothing.

"I'll be sixteen come summer," I say. "Sometimes I wonder if I'll ever be grown up and wise like him."

"He's not so wise."

"You don't think so?"

"He's just cocksure, which is not the same thing. It's the difference between veneer wood and solid. Same surface, but it's the inside matters. Eventually, that's what tells."

"Maybe Brother Joshua is solid wood," I say. I wonder at someone plain like Eddie daring to say such a thing. "You don't know."

"Maybe," he says. "But lately I don't trust nobody acting so certain."

Ruth Etta stirs, shifts off Eddie, and settles against the door. I push the lock button as quietly as I can.

"You doubt that boy because he's so certain?"

"Look how he called on the Lord to strike down the Viet Nam people."

"The Viet Cong is the ones he prayed against," I say, leaning forward, "the ones killing Americans."

"Some people say Americans shouldn't be over there to begin with."

"You don't believe them," I tell him. "Do you?"

"It's hard to know."

"Daddy says there's always a right to be found, if you sink down into yourself, below where your words are and look."

I feel weird, talking about Daddy's ways again, how he used his own good sense to work through things. I'd always figured there must be better ways, things I'd someday learn in college, things that let you sort what's true from what isn't. When I was young, I bragged on his ways. Now, though, I understand about our poverty, and I've turned cautious about passing them on. Folks who don't know me might think I'm not too bright for holding with such things. So I feel uneasy, telling Eddie, trusting he'll be fair.

We drive through a burst of snow. It's like we're inside one of

Ruth Etta's glass globe kingdoms, the kind with tiny trees and snow that swirls when you shake it. The flurry lasts for maybe two minutes. While it does, we don't talk.

"G.W. got his draft notice." Eddie's voice seems to well up from deep inside.

"When?" I ask over his shoulder.

"September," he says. "Only he didn't go."

Eddie stares out at the road. His reflection looks straight back at me.

"He has to go," I say. "The FBI will send him to jail."

"If they find him."

I've seen hippies and college radicals protesting and burning draft cards on TV. The Arabs turned Cassius Clay against his country, and now he's headed for prison. But this happens far off, New York or California. Stuff gets written on the wall behind the high school, but that's just ranting by a few strange birds, boys afraid to go. Eddie's brother isn't like that. "Your folks must know where he is."

He shakes his head. "Just me."

"Canada?"

"Don't ask," he says.

"Your parents must be . . ." I couldn't imagine.

"It hurt them bad. They say it's Communist liberals did it, the ones teaching him at college. They're worried what people think."

"I didn't know," I say.

"They're praying he'll change his mind before anyone finds out. Things won't stay that way much longer. Widicus promised if G.W. comes in now, they'll just let him go into the army and not prosecute. Otherwise, his name gets turned over to the FBI. Then it's criminal business, and his name's made public."

"You think he'll come in?"

"He loves our folks," Eddie says, "but he won't give hisself up to please them."

"I'm sorry," I tell him, and I mean it.

I'd always thought rich families like Eddie's, families with new cars all the time and children each with their own bedroom—I'd always figured they somehow managed to sidestep life's travails—that they had things better. I tell him that.

"Better?"

"Better than folks like us," I say. "No poverty."

"We scrape by." He looks at me, then back at the road. "Are your folks poor?" He asks it like he was asking did we drive Fords or Chevies.

I tell him about President Johnson, what he said about poverty being a disgrace and how Dad was getting us out and I was helping with the others. I didn't think I could ever tell anyone about this, but it has been forever on my mind. It feels safe telling Eddie now. He seems to be the open-minded kind. Maybe he won't think so badly of me.

We cross the bridge into Louisville under a cold starry sky, having left the flurries behind. Eddie says we'll be home in another couple hours. He opens his vent window and lights a cigarette, his first since Evansville. Ruth Etta throws a coat sleeve over her eyes to block out Louisville's lights, grumps once, and slips back into her quiet snoring.

Eddie says, "My mother's folks live in the hills back east. One summer she took G.W. and me back for a visit. I was maybe seven or eight. My great-grandparents lived in a cabin out past where the road ends. The old man still does. He works wood—builds furniture, caskets, sometimes a boat, always with hand tools. Mother says my knack for wood comes through his blood."

"I envy you, Eddie, having a special talent like that."

"You have a talent, Katy," he says. "You sing beautiful. Don't you know that?"

"Truly?" He must think I'm praise fishing, which I am not. Truth is, my voice is much too reedy. Anyone with ears can tell that. I'm just good at hiding it in the harmonies.

"Yes, I do think so," he says. "Besides, you have a warm and welcoming heart. Now that's something very special in you—

something I truly admire." A faint smile shows on Eddie's face. His neck seems to redden a bit. Or maybe it's the glow reflecting from his dashboard lights.

"Sometimes I think maybe I'll go back to Little Piney, sleep in my own bed again, just be who I always was, poverty or no. I'm doing what Daddy and me decided was best, and still I feel like there's something lost."

"Losing," Eddie says, and he smiles like there's a secret joke.

He is quiet for a while. I stare out the window, letting my mind drift. We are in the middle of dark countryside, miles from anywhere, still a ways from Spivey. So far, Ruth Etta's made the trip home without a single rest stop.

"Sometimes there's losing in every choice," Eddie says. He sounds dead serious. "You saw Widicus corner me at the singing?"

I'd almost forgot.

"This is between us, Katy." He says. "Just us."

My heart pounds. I want to say I'm just fifteen. Don't tell me that. But I want to listen too. For him.

"Okay," I say, and I scoot up again and lean close. My face is inches from his.

"Widicus gave me a message for G.W.," he whispers. "My brother comes in by next Tuesday, or I'll find my name at the top of the draft list."

"They can't," I say. "It's not fair!"

"No, it's not."

"Your brother, he'll have to—"

"G.W. doesn't have to do a damn thing, Katy."

I reach across and grab Eddie's shoulder. "But he wouldn't abandon you."

"Don't you see? That's what Widicus is counting on."

"I know he'll surrender."

"If I tell him," he whispers, and he touches my hand. "Maybe."

"Eddie!" I say. "You've got to tell him."

"He's doing what's right for him. Besides, my turn for the draft comes next year anyway. Who knows? Maybe the war will be won by then."

"He's the one should go now," I say. "Not you."

"I've turned it every which way in my mind." His voice is growing hoarse. "There's no good answers here," he says. "None."

Spivey is asleep when we finally get there, all the curtains drawn, the houses dark. The clock on Farmers First Bank says it's almost two in the morning.

Eddie stops the Mustang outside Embry's. I nudge Ruth Etta awake. She starts gushing apologies for being such a bad travel companion. And she reminds Eddie and me of our sacred oaths regarding the motel money. Then I take her arm and help her up the sidewalk and onto the front porch. Behind me, I hear the Mustang quietly drive away.

Ruth Etta goes straight off to bed and suggests I'd best do the same. But I linger around the front window, not ready yet for my long day to end, regardless of the clock.

Sure enough, Eddie Kenton drives up not five minutes later. I hurry out to the curb and thank him for returning my purse, which somehow got left in the Mustang's back seat. I ask him will he come take me for a ride tomorrow so we can talk more.

Overburden

"We're still eligible," Ben's wife, Sarah, calls from the veranda.

He mutes the sound on the *Tucson Morning News*. "AARP?" he asks. He means it as a joke, although his age—he is fifty-four—has been on his mind lately.

"Speak for yourself, old man," she says. Sarah is forty-five. She is also six months pregnant.

"What then?" Ben asks.

"The art and craft fair," she says. "The Appalachian Guild. We can still do their fair. We're invited."

She's taken her laptop outside this morning, along with her orange juice, her vitamins, and the single cup of coffee she allows herself now. She craves early sunshine and morning breezes. Soon enough she'll have to retreat as the day's heat builds. She'll do her morning yoga routine and then read and write e-mail out there, check her online art groups, and browse the political blogs—the lefties, the righties, and the directionless stirrers-up.

And lately, of course, she's frequenting maternity and mothering Web sites. Every day, it seems, she's telling him something new about pregnancy, nutrition, or baby IQs.

To Ben's way of thinking, he and Sarah have already done their share of populating the globe. True, theirs hasn't been your standard teamwork effort. More like tag team. His son, David, lone issue of his brief marriage to Cleome, has already made Ben a grandfather twice over. And Sarah's three girls from her first marriage are grown now, adults. The youngest, Lexie, is in her third year at Arizona State.

Ben goes to the kitchen to refill his coffee cup. He should cut back too. The caffeine can't be helping his blood pressure. He pours half a cup this time. In his head, he does the math again, the years, their ages. When this new child leaves the nest, Ben will be seventy-six. Seventy-six!

He takes his coffee out onto the veranda.

"Kate begs us," Sarah says. "They've got open spots." She runs her finger across the computer screen, selecting parts of the e-mail to read to him. "Saturday supper is at Harl and Minnie's house. Let's do go," she says. "You can sell books."

"Oh joy," Ben says. He'd prefer minor surgery.

"Don't be that way." She reaches for his hand. Morning sunlight shines on her upturned face. Pregnancy has brought back the freckles high on her cheeks and forehead, freckles that disappeared years ago. "It'll be such fun, seeing everyone," she says. "We can stop by reunion tree."

It has been too many years since he's been back to those mountains and valleys. Here in Arizona, mountains are rugged, imposing, layered in colors, but they're set on flat land and set too far apart to suit Ben. They'll never replace the embracing landscape he thinks of as home.

He takes Sarah's hand. "Should you fly?" he asks. "Will they even let you fly? You'll be what—seven and a half months, almost eight?"

"We'll need the van anyway," she says. "I'll take plenty of paintings, all but the gallery pieces."

"You'll be up for a trip like that?" he says. "Physically?"

She pulls her hand free. "I'm not fragile."

"I should be locked in my study writing, you know, not traipsing halfway across the country." He doesn't sound convincing and he knows it. Still, he's promised his editor a draft of the new novel by spring. Fifty-three rough pages, his halting start at the thing, are stacked on his desk. That's it. For weeks he's tried to add pages. They seem so scattershot though—the new pages hopelessly so. Nothing he adds seems to fit.

"You'll pull it out," she says. "Time away will do you good. You'll see."

"And the gallery, the fall show?"

"The girls can handle things." A look of doubt crosses Sarah's face now, the first he's seen this morning. "They must have cell phone service by now east of Adkins," she says. "Wouldn't you think?" Sarah's fingernails click the black plastic keys. She's asking Kate.

"The van," Ben says. "You know it's in no shape for a trip like that."

Sarah pushes the laptop away and turns to face him. "If you'd rather not go, say so."

"I'm just saying I wouldn't trust the van on a trip like that." The thing is ancient, a 1968 model, old even when they'd bought it, useful for local gallery deliveries these days and not much else. It hasn't left Pima County since hauling the five of them here on their move from Kentucky. That was more than a decade ago.

"We've got time," she says. "We can get it ready. It'll be fun. We can park and sleep anywhere along the way. It'll be like the old days."

"Us in that van," Ben says. "Won't we look like the aging hippies."

She goes back to the e-mail, starts typing, then stops again. "Yes," she says as if the idea just hit her. "Let's wear tie-dye."

All the way across New Mexico and Texas and into Oklahoma, they listen to the old music—Neil Young, Linda Ronstadt, the Eagles—on Ben's satellite radio. He'd managed to wire it into the van. He'd bolted a temporary hitch on the back, too, and rented a small U-Haul trailer to tow.

They trade off driving. With new tires, new spark plugs, and a rebuilt carburetor, the reborn van cruises dreamlike across the vast, flat land. Ben opens his window a couple of inches. Dry plains air blows in, swirls to the back. The smells of old straw and oil paints come forward to them. Out here his worries fade. He can almost believe they are young again, he and this beautifully ripe wife of his.

They park for the night at Orlie's Truck Stop outside Oklahoma City. They spread quilts between rows of boxed paintings and then make slow and gentle love to the blink of reflected neon lights, to the racket of idling diesel engines. Afterward they sleep in each other's embrace, the bulge of Sarah's belly a small mountain between them, legs languorous and tangled together.

Deep in the night, Ben feels their child move beneath his hand, a private moment, at once frightening and real, he and this unseen being—their child—almost touching, Sarah asleep and unaware.

Orlie's restaurant advertises breakfast twenty-four seven and free Wi-Fi. Ben orders wheat toast, low-cholesterol scrambled eggs, and coffee. Sarah fidgets with the menu. She twists a stray strand of hair across her face, tugs it under her nose like a moustache. She doesn't know what she wants, what she should or shouldn't have. Finally she settles on a blueberry nut muffin—no, cranberry—to go with her orange juice and coffee. He knows the signs. It'll be one of her hormonal mornings.

Ben buys the local newspaper from the box out front and leafs through it. Sarah boots up her laptop and composes an e-mail to oldest daughter Erin. She narrates the message to Ben as she types. She asks about things at the gallery. Did the Yuma clay artist ship his exhibit piece as promised? Was there anything in yesterday's mail from the Arizona Arts Commission? She thinks for a minute, fingernails tapping the table. Did the weekly payroll checks get mailed? She adds x's and o's and hits send as the waitress brings his toast and eggs, her muffin and juice.

They eat, and afterward Sarah checks for Erin's e-mail answer. Nothing.

"Relax," Ben tells her. "It's early there, just eight o'clock."

Sarah doesn't want to relax, and she tells him so. She opens her cell phone and punches in Erin's number. No answer. She closes the phone, opens it again, calls again, leaving voice mail this time. She sends a text message, telling her daughter to call, to check her voice mail for God's sake, check e-mail, just please please get in touch.

"She's a big girl," he says. Saying it doesn't seem to help.

Ben gasses up the van. He washes and squeegees the windshield, and with Sarah belted into the passenger seat again, he drives out to the interstate. He turns onto the eastbound ramp and accelerates into traffic. The van's tiny hood ornament is aimed like a gunsight into the rising, blinding sun.

Sarah's cell phone chimes. They're approaching Little Rock. She fishes the phone from her purse, checks the display. "Finally," she says. Ben kills the radio. Sarah, who lost her frantic edge an hour or two ago, answers the call on speaker setting.

All was well in Tucson, Erin tells them, amazingly, even with both of them not there. Erin majored in deft sarcasm. They shouldn't stress, she says, just relax and enjoy themselves, trust her to handle things. She'll call, she promises, if she needs anything, in the event something comes up that she can't handle. She's not twelve, she reminds them. She's twenty-five. Sarah says she knows.

"How's Igor?" Erin asks. She's already christened the baby, even though no one knows yet if it's a girl or boy. Absent this information, Erin has decided that the fates have ordained it will be the long-awaited, tormenting brother she and her sisters never had.

Sarah had all the genetic testing, of course, all the prudent screenings, once their biggest decision was made. Along the way, she's seen a dozen sonogram images too. Early on, she asked to be shown only the gender-indeterminate ones. Several are mounted on the side of their refrigerator now with tiny Monet magnets. One sonogram image even appears on their gallery's Web site, the employees' page. Igor is the name beside it.

Sarah lays a hand on top of her belly and shifts in the passenger seat. "Igor or Ivana, whichever," she says to Erin on the phone, "our tyke has taken up soccer in utero."

Erin goes away for a few seconds, comes back to tell them she has to take another call. Ben reaches across and switches on the radio again. He is ready for some bluegrass music. They'll cross the Mississippi River at Memphis in less than two hours. Kentucky lies not very far beyond. He finds the station. He puts his hand on his wife's hand, covers it with his on her belly. Then he reaches up and touches her hair, runs a finger along her cheek and chin. On the radio, Alison Krauss sings a high-speed, brokenhearted song. All the while, Sarah holds the cell phone open in front of her, looking at the thing, its bright screen a small lantern in her hand.

Ben loves living in Arizona, loves it more than he'd ever expected. Sarah does too. They love Tucson especially. They feel at home with its people, its cultural mix. They've even grown to love the harsh sun-bleached landscape, so unlike his native Kentucky and yet somehow inspiring. His writing has flourished in the desert. At least it has until recently.

Still, returning to Kentucky is coming home for Ben. Already he feels the change, a new lightness, this shedding of another skin that might or might not be his. He grew up here, after all, came of age in the Appalachian foothills. Family members going back four generations are buried in graveyards around Burkitt County. Their claims on the place make it his too.

Sarah has napped. She's done some quick yoga stretches at a rest stop. Now she drives the trip's final leg.

The van tires hiss on wet asphalt. Even though daylight is fading, even though a misty drizzle falls now from an overcast sky, the lush greens of the countryside sliding by overwhelm Ben—the distant hills, the fields of tall grasses, the broad-leaved trees, everything so green. Scents of damp earth and wet vegetation seem to be everywhere. Trees are showing the first fall colors—a hint of bright maple reds, coming yellows among the tulip poplars, the rusted orange-brown of oaks. Living in the desert, he's forgotten how brilliant Octobers can be.

Sarah drives through Burkitt County. These are familiar roads and buildings. Familiar names appear on signs everywhere. He feels cut loose from the world now, untethered, floating free across the land.

"Rain," Sarah says. She switches the wipers on full speed and leans forward to see the sky. "Must be an outdoor craft fair nearby."

They'd met at the Appalachian Art and Craft Fair, Ben's first, eighteen Octobers ago. Back then, the fall fair was held on the wooded hillside along McKesson Creek.

Ben wrote freelance articles for *Kentucky Crafts Magazine*, for the *Artisan's Way*, for the *Lexingtonian*, or for anyone else who'd buy what he wrote. He'd lined up six artists to interview that weekend at the fair, one being Sarah Waters. At the time, he was also working on his first novel, bogged down irretrievably somewhere near the middle of it. Everything in his life seemed a muddle then. Ben and Cleome had split the year before. She'd moved to Knoxville and taken their son with her. She'd hooked up with an East Coast cowboy who taught country dance classes—line dancing, country swing, whatever was popular. Nothing Cleome did had ever made sense to him.

Sarah's paintings were all pastorals then, rustic scenes of rolling countryside, small streams, all bright yellows, greens, and blues. Her outfit for art and craft fairs—plain shoes, white bonnet, long-hemmed gray dress, and a brightly colored silk scarf tied at her neck—suggested the early Kentucky Shakers of Union Village and Pleasant Hill. In fact, Sarah was a city girl whose home and studio were in Cincinnati. She dreamed even then, she told Ben, of opening her own gallery, a place to show and sell work by artists she admired to people who would appreciate it. He remembers thinking how completely in control of her life Sarah seemed to be, how calm she was at the center.

Sarah's three girls had come down from Cincinnati with her for the fair. All afternoon, or so it seemed, Erin carried little Lexie up the hill and back, carried her on her hip like a mother would. Four-year-old Brie hid behind the back flap of Sarah's open-sided tent. She peered out at Ben, this strange man with a thick notebook and so many questions. He saw her watching other people too, the ones browsing the large hanging paintings and the smaller ones in bins. Before the afternoon ended, Brie was mimicking Ben, doing whatever he did. She brought him fistfuls of colorful leaves she'd gathered too. He remembers that especially.

Ben photographed Sarah with her work. He photographed her in front of her tent, which was shaded by a giant red oak tree, the tallest on the hillside. He photographed her on the woodchip path, posing her with Mercy Mountain in the background. Photos, he told her, make an article easier to place. In his viewfinder, Sarah seemed lit from within, that young face shaped by prominent cheekbones and animated by those expressive hazel-green eyes.

That afternoon, he stayed with Sarah longer than he'd planned. At one point, an acorn—cap, twig, and all—dropped from the red oak. It plunked off his shoulder and splashed into his coffee, giving Brie a serious giggle fit. It was a sign, Sarah said, an omen of good luck.

Ben asked everything he could conceivably need to know for an artist's profile. And even after all his questions were asked and answered, he still found it hard to leave.

One question he didn't know to ask, one bit of information Sarah didn't volunteer, either, concerned her husband, Levon, and their divorce. The decree would be final in ten days. This Ben learned a month later when he phoned to fact-check the finished piece. As soon as Sarah told him—he always says this in the retelling—he knew the direction things would take.

It's their story now, the one they tell when asked how they met. They tell it the same, the details of that day—the craft fair, the lucky acorn, Brie's bouquet of bright leaves, and their immediate attraction. That day hadn't felt like a first meeting to either of them. They like to think of it as a reunion of long-separated souls, a kind of mutual redeeming. And the red oak, in their retelling, they call the "reunion tree."

She drives on toward Adkins, the rain now a light drizzle.

The fair hasn't been held along McKesson Creek for years—for nearly a decade, according to Kate. This will be their first time back since it moved, though, and Ben finds himself anticipating disappointment, a kind of reflex lately, just thinking of the change.

Sarah steers the van into an open grass field behind Adkins Community Hall and parks among the cluster of other vans, trucks, and travel trailers. The rain has stopped, but there are no stars overhead, no moon to see by. In the open field, Ben can make out the shapes of several scattered tents. Those with lights inside glow like party lanterns. A dozen portable toilets, tan and dark blue, line the nearby fence. A single flashlight beam drifts across the field.

"Looks like the place," Sarah says. She sets the brake and switches off the headlights. "I wonder if Kate's here." She peers through the windshield and out across the field, squinting as though she might see in the dark.

"It's so flat," Ben says, opening his door. "No trees. You won't have shade."

She glares at him. "Say something positive," she tells him. "Say something fast before I hit you." Her tone is light, but he knows her message is serious.

Immediately, he regrets what he's said, that reflex attitude of his. "It's quit raining," he tells her in the cheeriest voice he can summon. "And it's rained enough to keep the dust down tomorrow." Two positives there, and she'd asked for only one.

"Better," Sarah says. He's off the hook for now. She leans across the seat, unlatches the glove compartment, and gropes inside for a flashlight. "The gate guard must have the fair layout and exhibitor list."

In the morning they haul paintings and hinged display boards out to where Kate's husband, Eddie Kenton, has set up a tent for Sarah. Ben handles the heavy stuff. By eight o'clock, the field is alive with activity, more exhibitors arriving every minute, tents blooming on their poles, ropes strung, metal stakes hammered into the ground.

At ten o'clock the gates open. Sarah has her tall folding chair set up beside the tent, and she's taken her seat. She wears a muumuu, tentlike and brightly tie-dyed, a sweater on top until the morning chill is gone. She left the old Shaker outfit in Tucson. Sarah rarely wears it anymore. Wearing it now would be ludicrous anyway—she'd pointed this out while packing—ludicrous not only because the fit would be snug but also because Shaker women were celibate by vow. One would never appear in public so obviously pregnant.

"People nowadays won't know that," Lexie had scoffed. "They won't care."

"I would," she'd told Lexie, and that was that.

Kate Kenton's tent is next to Sarah's, her green-glazed clay pieces teeming with toads, frogs, pink octopi, and blue walking fish.

A young woman with serious ear metal, taped-together shoes, and no makeup is set up on the other side. Her hair is streaked in crayon colors—red, yellow, and blue. Her name, she says, is Amber Peach, a name Ben is convinced is invented. Smoked glasses are propped on her forehead. She drops them into position when she lights the flame on her butane torch. In the flame, she pulls strands from colored glass rods, building up decorative glass beads, demonstrating how it's done.

Farther down the trail, Chester Ford rives shingles from red oak. His wood mallet strikes the froe rhythmically. The wood splits as Ford twists the tool, then tears the wood apart in his powerful hands. Across the way, two more new faces—a bearded photographer in a leather hat and a stocky woman with children's wooden puzzles cut with a scroll saw.

And beyond her are the McKessons—Harlan and Minnie. Ben had helped them set up their tent, once Sarah's paintings were all carted out. Now Harl, dressed in bib overalls and permanently stooped, splits fine white oak strips with a penknife, while Minnie, plump as ever, weaves the splits into traditional baskets so small they fit inside half shells of hens' eggs. They've been basket makers forever. They'd have to be older than seventy-six, Ben tells himself. Much older. Maybe eighty.

It is a sparse morning crowd. Between customers, Ben sits in Sarah's chair while she walks across to talk with Minnie, to catch up on news and gossip. Sarah opens her sweater, pulls the muumuu snug, and turns sideways to show her shape. She clamps a hand over Minnie's mouth, laughing, to keep her—Ben has no doubt of this—from guessing the child's gender. Not that Minnie could know for certain. No one could. But Minnie has been a midwife too, been one forever, and Ben thinks that her guess might just mean something.

Around noon, the sun comes out. The morning chill is gone now. In the parking lot, Ben orders two walleye sandwiches from a food vendor. While he waits, he goes over to the water fountain beside the building. It's dry. It's been disconnected, he sees. Nearby, men from the Adkins Rescue Crew relax on the back bumper of their emergency vehicle. They're smoking and trading stories. The community well turned acid, one tells Ben. Bad sulfur. They're hoping it's temporary. "It's bottled water, Cokes, or nothing," the guy says. Ben goes back to pick up the wrapped sandwiches. He grabs napkins too and buys bottled water.

He holsters the bottles in his jacket pockets. The sandwiches are warm in his hands. Ben can feel his mood lift. Maybe it's the sunlight on his shoulders and face, he thinks. Maybe it's the bustling crowd. Or maybe the whole secret is to shrug off everything else and find something purposeful to do—like getting fish sandwiches and bringing them back. Maybe that's all it takes.

Eddie Kenton tosses car keys to his wife, Kate. "The roads to the McKesson place are so messed up," he tells Ben, "even my GPS gets it wrong."

It's five o'clock. The fair crowd, not very large all day, has dwindled to nothing. An hour ago, Minnie left for home. All afternoon she'd worried that Darby, the daughter-in-law she'd left in charge at the house, might forget something, that she might not have the meal ready and set out right. She wouldn't hear "don't worry."

"You all can follow me out," Kate says. "It's not far. Or ride along. Your choice."

Sarah says they'll ride along before Ben has a chance to say otherwise. He feels as though she's been loaned out all day. He'd like his wife back, even if only for those few minutes, the two of them in their van, riding. Amber Peach says she'd like to ride along too. Eddie Kenton and Harl McKesson will finish buttoning up and anchoring the tents. They'll follow in Harl's truck.

Ben gets the wine they've brought from Tucson—three bottles in a pocketed cloth sack—brings it over to the Kentons' Escalade, and climbs in. The seats in back are more comfortable than anything in Ben and Sarah's living room, the leather fragrant and soft. Thick paper covers the floor mats. The seatbelts are folded in place and bound in paper bands like hotel toilet seats. "We're the first to ride back here?" he asks.

"You are," Kate says brightly. "Hope you like it." A bowl of something heavily seasoned with curry is beside her on the seat.

Sarah buckles her belt. "What's not to like?" she says.

Ben leans forward and says, "If you don't mind, we'll sleep back here tonight." Kate says they should make themselves at home. She'll teach the locks their thumbprints. They can come and go as they please. He was kidding. She might be. He can't tell. He could never get comfortable here anyway, couldn't sleep here, despite what he just said. Too much luxury unsettles him.

The road over to McKesson Creek is familiar. It's the road to the place the fair was held years ago—the creek, the hillside and wooded path, their reunion tree. If he remembers right, it's not far beyond Harl and Minnie's house. If Sarah feels up to it, they'll hike there after supper, look around, and indulge their nostalgia just a bit.

Kate steers right onto the road that parallels the creek. It's wider than Ben remembers, the asphalt rippled and rutted. Within a half mile, the road climbs and the world changes. Tulip poplar trees, redbuds, and magnolias vanish. Their green and gold canopy gives way to a landscape of endless stumps and mammoth log stacks on the denuded hillside.

And then, quite startlingly, the road becomes a narrow land bridge across a vast expanse of drab, sculpted tablelands, gray rock and rubble everywhere. It could be Mars or the moon. Some distance away, a rusted yellow hulk of machinery lies on its side, its skid tracks down an embankment still visible. A wide, basin-shaped pond is dug into the plateau below. It brims with an inky green liquid. Ben guesses that the pond is two hundred yards across or maybe more. Size and distance out here are hard to judge.

"Copper mining?" Amber asks. She's says she's seen pictures in National Geographic.

"Kentucky coal," Kate tells her, "the world's best. They took out this mountain in under three years."

Sarah moves closer to the window. "This mess was a mountain?" Ben can feel it too, the desolation here, the sense that something beautiful and sacred has been defiled. He takes her hand in his.

"They're coming back in the spring," Kate says, "to start reclamation of the land. They'll plant special grasses and all that."

It is behind them now. They are back among magnolias and hemlock trees, back on nature's land, nearby trees flying by as the Escalade skirts a steep hillside. The road forks at a small brick house, abandoned now. Ben recognizes it, though, remembers it and knows where he is again. They veer right, following McKesson Creek.

A minute later, Kate steers onto a roadside gravel patch and stops. A sway footbridge spans the creek. On the other side, Minnie McKesson waves from the porch of a large, two-story hodgepodge of a house.

Kate, carrying her bowl, crosses the bridge first, crosses it cautiously. Amber follows, and then Sarah and Ben, toting the wine sack. He feels the rhythmic bridge-deck motion in his legs, in his feet. He pauses midspan while the motion settles. Below, the creek banks are wild with insects and tangled blackberry vines. The creek bottom, bedrock shale, is nearly dry. What little water flows is the color of rust.

The porch wraps around the house on three sides. The wood sounds hollow under his feet. Rattan chairs and table are on one side, a swing on the other. Wind chimes dangle at each corner, and random-weave reed baskets hang from every porch post. The baskets have small openings with perches for nesting birds.

Minnie's daughter-in-law has forgotten to proof the yeast, much to Minnie's distress. There's no bread yet to go with the meal, she tells them. There won't be for another two hours. Beer, cold drinks, pretzels, and Vienna sausages will have to tide everyone over until the new dough rises, until her bread finally bakes, she says. Then the real meal begins.

Ben sets the sack of bottles on the table. "Sarah and I are going over to the old fairgrounds." He means it as an invitation to the others.

"You won't recognize it," Harl says, coming in. Eddie Kenton follows him, the screen door slamming behind.

"It's been mined too?" Ben asks.

"There's no coal in a valley to mine," Harl says. "It's all layered in mountains."

"What then?" Sarah asks.

Harl hangs his cap on a wall peg and runs a hand through what's left of his hair. "My brother's got no sense. His kids neither. They sold their land. This was eight or ten years ago." He gives an apologetic kind of shrug, an embarrassed one. "It's where the over-burden from Mercy Mountain got dumped."

"Overburden," Ben says.

"Mountaintop," Harl says, "all of it down to the coal. They cut the trees. They blast everything loose, all the rock down to the coal seam, all the stuff between them. They load it up and haul it off, dump it in valleys to get it out of the way."

"The blasting cracked our foundation," Minnie says, "cracked it in four places. Our well went muddy for a month. Now it's bone dry."

"The trees too?" Sarah asks. "They get dumped?" Ben knows the tree on her mind. She's sitting now. She looks flushed, tired.

Harl says, "Some logs they'll truck to a sawmill. Most just get dumped in valleys though. Good lumber trees get buried with everything else."

"I'll drive you over there," Eddie says, "if you want to see." He's got car keys in his hand. "Ben? Sarah? Harl?"

"You go," Sarah tells Ben. She needs to be off her feet. Besides, she's got catching up to do.

"You're sure?" he asks.

"Go," she says again, waving him away. A tight smile is on her face.

The women stay, and the three men go.

Weeds and bushes lean in from the sides of the road, narrowing it. Eddie drives the centerline so branches won't scratch his new Escalade. At a barricade of old guardrails, the road abruptly ends.

The men get out, clamber over the bent metal, and walk another thirty yards. The pavement is covered in leafed twigs, small branches, and acorns. Ben bends and picks up an acorn. For luck, he tells himself, rolling it in his hand.

They come into the open. The land drops away sharply to a vast, rocky plateau seventy or eighty feet below. Sprigs of grass grow in clumps here and there. A steep gravel path leads down from where they stand.

Nothing is familiar now.

"Look like your Arizona," Harl asks, "the desert?"

"Hell no," Ben says. Maybe it does to someone who's never been there. The desert he knows is a living thing. This is desolation.

Eddie points toward a small rise a mile or more away. "Mercy Mountain," he says, "used to be over there."

Harl points almost straight ahead, "Over there, more to the west," he says. "This was my brother's land. I ought to know."

"And the hillside where the fair was held?" Ben asks. The two men point at different angles.

"Wait," Eddie says. He hurries back to the car and returns a minute later with a GPS in his hand. "This little beauty's got a topo map."

The three men stare at the device while it boots up and locates satellites. When it does, it tells them that they're at the end of Highway 1344. True enough.

Eddie touches screen settings. Topographic lines are overlaid, along with feature names. It's the only topography the thing knows, the old names, what existed before. He aligns directions on the screen by the setting sun. "Mercy Mountain," he says, pointing at the screen and then pointing at nothing visible in the distance.

Harl looks at the screen. He squints out at the landscape as if trying to see a mountain there.

"And McKesson Creek," Eddie says. His finger snakes a course, left to right, not too far away. "Down two hundred feet from what you see."

They take the path down, take it slowly, Eddie in front of old Harl and Ben behind. Then they start hiking out across the rock and rubble. The ground is hard-packed, solid underfoot. The grass sprigs are dry, the blades sharp. They look sparser up close. The scrub bushes are like nothing Ben has ever seen. In his hand, he feels the acorn come apart, the cap and the nut, and realizes that he must have been squeezing it.

The men walk several hundred yards. Eddie veers off to one side. "Okay," he says, stopping. "I'm standing in McKesson Creek now." He stomps his foot as if splashing water. A small cloud of dust comes up. He's clearly enjoying this. Ben and Harl go over and take a look. On the display, their position is on the creek trace, but wobbly. Harl asks why.

"Our altitude," Eddie says. "The consensus of the satellites is that we're airborne, soaring over this valley. It's programmed to expect only ground locations."

Ben tries to imagine the stream buried down there, somewhere beneath his feet, all the trees dumped there, the soil, and on top of it all—what was all that rock called—the overburden? It hurts just thinking about it, everything turned upside down and destroyed. He's relieved now that Sarah didn't come. She'll remember the place as it was.

"Can't no one make this right again," Harl says. "Can't no one ever put it back the way the good Lord made it." He kicks at the packed rubble with the toe of his boot. "And they'll keep coming back to these mountains, taking more every year. The only thing that'll stop them is when there's none left to take."

Ben can feel the old man's anger. He feels it as a tightness in his chest, as something sour high in his throat. He moves close to Eddie, examines the topo map, the ghost places on the display. "The hillside," he says, "where the craft fair would set up." He touches a place on the map. "Here?"

Harl and Eddie study the screen, the hills contours there, and agree it would have to be. The sun is low now, their shadows long, but supper won't be ready for some time. "I'm going to hike over there," Ben tells them.

"Why? Walk a mile that way," he says, pointing, "or walk two miles that way, you won't see nothing but more of this."

"I've come this far," Ben says.

Eddie hands him the GPS. "We'll be back at the car."

Ben hikes across the cut rises and falls of the stepped plateau. It's tiring work, slopes and side slopes, every step uneven, ankle-twisting, each footfall not quite where he anticipates. What looks flat at a distance is uneven up close. The screen blip moves too, inching toward the contours of a phantom hillside where their reunion tree once grew.

It takes longer than he expected, but finally Ben reaches the place—what he thinks, he believes, he hopes must be the place. He kicks with the back of his heel, digging into the surface, wedging out a rut in the hard pack. When the hole is ankle deep, he drops the acorn and cap in. He kneels, and with both hands, he scoops loose material back over top and pats it there. It's too rocky. He knows that. But it's all he can think to do.

Ben gets up and starts back across the barren ground. He's eager to be gone, wants never to see this place again.

The sun is down, the sky a deepening blue. Ben follows the two men across the bridge and watches them go up onto the porch. He pauses on the path and tries to imagine telling Sarah what he's seen. On the porch, Minnie's wind chimes sound their mystical, random tunes. So much devastation nearby, and still the scent of baked bread drifts out to him.

Inside, Sarah will tell him that her labor has started, early pains, but unmistakable. There's no need to rush, she'll say, but they shouldn't delay, either, getting to the hospital. It's only a matter of time. Yes, it's five weeks early, maybe six, but their future, she'll assure him, is most certainly happening now.

So Exotic

"He's so exotic," Quilla whispers to Rita, "don't you think?" She's talking about Georgi Vijov, of all people.

Most mornings Quilla Coe shows up at Rita's Huddle In Café around nine-thirty. The morning rush lets up about then, and Rita can use a break. She'll pour coffee for herself and take tea to Quilla in booth six. For a few minutes, Rita will sit, shoes off, feet propped on the opposite seat, and they'll talk. Not long ago it occurred to Rita that she and Quilla are friends. She marvels at this. They're such an unlikely pair.

Quilla is built slender, her features unremarkably plain. At thirty-seven, she's two years younger than Rita and still single. Rita is a generous size. The features of her face are rounded, her makeup boldly applied. Rita married young. She's been married twice.

Quilla, a late only child, grew up in town. Rita lived in a double-wide out on Ponder Road, lived there with her mother, three half sisters, and a stepbrother. In school, Rita thought Quilla weird, so bookish, so mousy looking. Back then, she imagined that girls like Quilla envied her, all daring with the boys, smoking fresh-dried weed like Marlboro Lights.

Rita looks at things differently now. She's older and settled down.

"Exotic?" Rita's hands smooth her apron front. "He sure is, honey."

99

Everyone in town thinks Georgi Vijov is at least a little strange. Some call him crazy. Rita considers him borderline weird, even allowing for his being an artist, a foreign one at that. He's not the usual kind of catalog handsome. He's the other kind. She feels a vague uneasiness now, hearing Quilla mention him, her neck prickly and warm. She imagines his skin, pale beneath the tattered T-shirt he always wears. Tattoos wouldn't surprise her.

Vijov appeared in town six months ago. He eats breakfast often at the Huddle In. He comes in early after painting all night, his clothes and shoes spattered, the skin of his hands cracked and chalky and smelling of turpentine. His hair is a corkscrewed, paint-flecked mess. Curls snake from beneath his black wool cap. Vijov is always alone, always carrying some book in those sinewy hands. He never sits at the counter. Instead, he takes a booth for himself, the one in the corner if it's empty. He orders three eggs scrambled, biscuits, no gravy or meat, whole-wheat toast, a large orange juice, and coffee. Lots of coffee. He asks for refills, a half dozen sometimes. After weeks of this, Rita pointed to the pot on the warming plate. "Help yourself from now on," she told him.

Vijov does. He has no qualms. He's short on manners too. Rita wonders if everyone where he comes from doesn't tip. For certain, Vijov doesn't. Never.

Rita talks to him though, in a neighborly way. Her new husband, Price, calls her broad-minded, and she likes to think she's that way. It's her name on the place after all—Rita's Huddle In Café. She wants her customers to be glad they came, wants them smiling as they leave. She believes that every customer smile speaks well of her, of how she runs the place. Respect came late to Rita. She worked hard for it and worries about losing it in some careless moment.

Vijov isn't the smiling kind though. Maybe he saw too much misery in his country. He's new to America—he told her this months ago—coming here from Belarus. She thinks that's part of Russia. Or close to Russia. He uses dictionary words by the bushel. His

English is strangely accented, and he talks in quick bursts. Rita thinks this strange, a foreigner speaking English so fast. Listening, she works just to keep up.

Quilla looks into her cup. "Would you consider him handsome?" She traces the rim of the cup with a manicured finger.

"Handsome?" Rita says. "I suppose." She imagines the sunburned shoulders of another, a boy. He's a memory, just a flash in her mind.

"He's young," Rita says. "Vijov."

"Is he?" Quilla leans closer. Her splash of sweet scent fills the booth.

"Twenty-three," Rita says. Another flash, the young boy with no shirt, his face familiar, but she can't remember his name. She follows him, walks into a field tall with tobacco blooms. Rita draws a quick breath and combs fingers through her hair.

"He came into the bank yesterday," Quilla says. She works at Farmers First Bank, which is directly across Main Street. She's assistant to the manager. Five days a week she's there at seven, two hours before the bank opens to customers. She's one of the last to leave too, one of the pair that locks up. She's told Rita that she likes being counted on. She wears low heels and suits with straight skirts, the kind only slender women dare wear. Her walk is a tentative kind. Her skirt barely moves on her delicate frame. Rita envies women like Quilla, their bone structure, all the clothes they can wear.

"Vijov?" Rita says.

"I saw from my office window."

Rita sets her cup down, looks across at her.

Quilla says, "It's got one-way glass."

Something inside Rita squirms. She remembers her uncle's burley field, tobacco worms everywhere, long and green and thick as a man's finger.

"He studied the interest rate board," Quilla says, "for the longest time. He thumbed through the brochures, he wrote on a deposit slip, and when he finished, he tied a tiny noose in the pen chain. Finally, he turned toward me. I know he couldn't see me through that glass, and still, I stepped quickly behind the drape. When I looked again, he was gone."

"You think he's up to something?"

Quilla glances around. Two old men nurse Cokes at the counter. Otherwise, the place is empty. From her purse, Quilla takes a crumpled slip of paper. She smoothes it with her hand and slides it across for Rita to see.

"Please," she says, laying her hand on Rita's arm, "please don't tell anyone." The hand is like ice.

On the paper, four sketched lines, single strokes. Rita's eyes want them at first to be letters, ornate letters of some foreign language. Then she sees their pattern. One line is hair, another forehead and nose, one lips and jaw, and the last the curve of a long and graceful neck. It's a woman's profile, Quilla's profile. If she'd handed Rita a photograph, it couldn't have been a truer likeness.

"Vijov drew this?"

She nods. "Turn it over."

On the other side, printed in black block letters—"I see you watch me."

"Good Lord, Quilla," Rita says. "He's paranoid."

"But I do," Quilla says quickly. "I watch him. Not obviously, of course. How could he know?" She folds the sketch, slips it back into her purse. "Unless he reads minds?"

"Why him?" Rita's voice is a whisper. "Why Vijov? He's not exactly your kind." Rita remembers how it felt, her bare feet on plowed ground, how the sun's warmth felt, rising up to her from uneven earth.

Quilla's gaze goes away. "He's so exotic. Enticing. Strange." She finishes her tea, dabs a napkin at the corners of her mouth, and folds it into the cup. "It's like if I touch him maybe I'll light up too."

Rita takes the cup. "This isn't you," she says.

"Maybe it is." Quilla stares at her now, stares as she stands. "Maybe it's time I find out."

A week later, four customers are lined up at Rita's cash register. She's ringing them up when Georgi Vijov comes in. By the time she gives the last one his change, Vijov has settled into the corner booth and poured coffee for himself.

"I am having my usual order, which you know," he calls to her.

She waves and starts to take him a menu but realizes he's ordered without one. She wants a reason to go over, to talk. Over the past week, she's seen Quilla across the street. She hasn't stopped once at the Huddle In though. Rita wonders if she's embarrassed about telling so much, acting like a schoolgirl about Vijov, acting brave and not following through. Everyone oversteps themselves sometimes. Rita has, more times than she likes to admit. You just keep moving on. That's the secret. Don't stop. She worries that, embarrassed, Quilla is avoiding her now.

Rita tries to remember if she wiped down Vijov's booth table. Her doubt is reason enough. She grabs a table rag and heads for the corner booth.

Vijov is reading a tattered paperback book, *Prophesies of Nostradamus*, holding it in one hand as he sips from his cup, which he balances in the palm of the other. Tiny earphones are buttoned into his ears. The wires twitch with the thudding bass beat. Vijov's attention is on the book, and for a moment, Rita is unsure if he knows that she's there. But then, still reading, he lifts his elbows for her to wipe the table.

He smells of paint oils, a smooth aroma that she feels at the back of her throat. He's not a small man, but the book appears bulky in his hands. His fingers are long, like a piano player's. Two extend like sticks up the book's creased spine and back.

"More coffee?" she says.

He lifts his cup, tugs the dangling wire so his earplugs pop out. Quilla's right. The guy is handsome, in an exotic sort of way. Rita realizes then that she didn't bring the pot. "I'll get it," she says.

She returns and refills his cup. "Eggs will be out in a minute."

His long fingers grab her wrist, and he pulls her closer. "Quilla says that she confides only to you."

"We're friends," Rita says and pulls away.

His hand snaps open, relaxes, makes an apologizing gesture in the air. "She tells you that she comes to my room, that she consents to pose for me. No?"

"She does?" There's no way for Rita to hide her surprise.

He sits back now, sips his coffee. "Quilla Coe is this perfect model for one artist to have."

"How in the world," she says. "How did you convince her?"

"No one must convince a flower to bloom."

"But Quilla . . ."

"She becomes who she is," Vijov says, "which is as it should be."

Okay, Rita thinks. There is something magnetic about this guy. But she's known Quilla for years. And this seems so unlike her.

"I see you worry for her," Vijov says. "I will tell Quilla that she must comfort her friend's mind. This she must do soon."

He plugs his earphones in again, flips pages with those creepy fingers, and folds back into himself. The egg plate gets a nod, as does the check, which he pays, a distant stranger again.

"He is so bizarre," Quilla says. Rita brings her a slice of lemon meringue pie. "You have no idea."

Rita really doesn't want to hear this. And she does.

Two short hours ago, Vijov said he would tell her to comfort Rita's mind. Here she is, dressed primly and buttoned high. She's paler than Rita remembers. She looks slimmer than before.

"He said you pose for him," Rita says with all the nonchalance she can muster.

A smile bursts across Quilla's face like never before. It looks good on her, Rita thinks, but it's so unlikely, this smile. "It's not what you think, Rita."

"No. I'm sure it's not." Rita imagines prim Quilla kneeling in a field of tall tobacco, the plants' wide leaves wet with dew, the drops heavy and tinted with leached nicotine. Her cotton dress is loose at the neck and damp with sweat.

Quilla says, "It's hard to explain. But Georgi insists I ease your mind on this."

"No need." Rita stands to leave, hoping Quilla will stop her, hoping she won't.

"No. Please sit. I want you to know." Her hand on Rita's arm reminds her of Vijov's bold gesture. Her hand feels different though, not as dry or insistent.

"You don't owe me."

"It's okay." Quilla's smile is back. "Just let me tell it."

Rita slides back onto the booth seat. Quilla's face has lost some color, but her eyes seem to shimmer. Her hands move now, move freely in ways they haven't before. Her lips seem fuller, her tongue is a brighter shade of red. Or, Rita wonders, is it only her pale complexion making it seem that way? No, she decides, Vijov is right. She's bloomed. She's more delicate now. More vulnerable too.

"I wear clothes." Quilla's words are a sudden blurt. "When I pose, I'm not nude."

"Costumes?"

Rita remembers the tiny blue flowers on her long-ago, cotton print dress, how it hung on her. She would wear it off her shoulders, the breeze rippling it around her, so many summers ago.

"This is difficult," Quilla says. "Georgi insists that I wear what makes me comfortable. He paints the essence, not the body."

Lost between memory and this moment, Rita doesn't understand. Her confusion must show on her face.

"Okay," Quilla explains. "It sounds bizarre, Rita, but try to be open." Her gaze feels intense. "It's telepathic, what he does, a convergence of auras and psychic harmonies."

Rita studies her friend's face and tries to imagine what goes on in Vijov's room.

"Trust me on this." Quilla extends her hand. Her eyes seem to ask for understanding too. "He has me think things—only think them. Nothing more."

Rita feels a warmth, like July sun on her neck. "Things like what?"

"He's an artist. His ideas might sound weird if I told them. The thoughts aren't mine. Not really. They're just what I'm thinking as his model. It's like wearing someone else's clothes for a photograph. Except it's thoughts."

"Uh huh," Rita says. This isn't what she expected.

"Georgi receives the thought's energy," she says, "and he paints from that."

"The energy," Rita says.

She remembers a quilt in that moment, a log cabin pattern, an old quilt carried by her and the boy. They carry it between them swagged like a hammock. She can still taste his sweat on her tongue. Fain. John Fain—she remembers his name now. John Fain, the boy who said, "Come away with me," the one who taught her regret.

"I know it sounds strange," Quilla's voice is saying, louder now and strained. "It's hard to visualize. I concentrate and repeat the image he gives me. When I feel myself fade away, that's when he can connect with the energy. You should see him, Rita, the frenzy when he paints. He's in this high-energy trance. You'd expect paint on the canvas would be layered inches thick by the time he's done." Her laugh is a rich and throaty sound.

"You've seen the finished paintings?" Rita says.

In her mind, the sweet aroma of burley blooms seems to be everywhere. It's a warm-July-night cotton-candy kind of smell. She remembers the blooms, long and pink, the field alive with flights of hummingbirds. She remembers the buzz of wings, how they felt near her skin, how her hair moved in their whisper-breeze. She remembers red throats throbbing too, thin beaks probing ecstatically in that field of pink deep-trumpet blooms.

Quilla's gaze has gone away. "He keeps the canvas draped," she is saying. "He doesn't want to pollute my mental imaging with his representations of them. Sometimes he yells and curses as he paints, but once he's finished, he seems pleased. At first, I was too tight. My full essence didn't come through, and Georgi couldn't connect. It frustrated him. Now we perform a psychic sieve before starting, and everything works much better."

Rita studies Quilla's face. She tries to imagine what a psychic sieve might be.

Quilla says, "I know this sounds bizarre. If only you were there, if only you saw him."

"No thanks." Rita feels uneasy now, misplaced.

Come away with me—that's what John Fain had said all those years ago. And still the tug is there, the wondering, what if, if only she'd dared. Rita craves distance from Quilla, just for now, some solitude. Quilla demands unwelcome closeness, too much familiarity suddenly, this woman so unlike her.

"I don't mean you'd actually watch," Quilla says. "This is personal between Georgi and me."

"You look tired," Rita says, and she picks up her cup to go. "Are you getting your sleep?"

"It's exhausting. But I feel fantastic. Most mornings I nap on the office couch." She fingers her purse. "I've missed having my morning coffee with you."

Rita says, "I worry about you."

Quilla stands now too. "What I have with Vijov might seem perilous. Sometimes it frightens me too. But it's been miraculous," she says, touching her chest, "in here, like being born. It's so bizarre, Rita. You can't know."

"Come back," Rita tells her. "Come at least once a week."

Walking away, she glimpses Quilla's reflection in the front window. She sees her open her purse and pinch a pill between finger and thumb. She places it on her tongue, places it there like sacrament, then stretches her neck like a bird and swallows.

Weeks pass. Sometimes Rita sees Quilla enter or leave the bank. She's skinny now. Even her fitted skirts hang on her. She doesn't come for pastry or tea.

One day a young teller at the counter mentions Quilla's name. "Is she sick?" Rita asks.

"She quit," the girl says, looking up from her conversation. "Yesterday. The woman simply doesn't care anymore."

The man beside her says, "She's sick. That's what I think."

That afternoon, Rita phones Quilla's house. There is no answer, not even a machine. Over the next few days, Rita phones a dozen times. She buys a card and writes inside that she hopes Quilla is well, and then she mails it.

One evening Rita knocks on Quilla's front door. Inside, a dog barks. No one answers though.

The next morning, Georgi Vijov comes into the Huddle In. A patchy growth of whiskers frames his face now. He slides onto a stool at the counter, even though his corner booth is open. Earbuds pump music straight to his brain.

"Coffee," he orders too loudly. His wool cap, pulled low, can't hide a bruise near his temple. Today his lanky fingers aren't paint-flecked.

Rita slides a cup across the counter. "I haven't seen Quilla Coe lately," she says.

His eyes seem vacant. There's no turpentine smell today, a hint of rosewater instead. She wonders if he heard her.

Rita touches his hand, touches it lightly for attention. It flips and recoils like a startled animal. In that instant Rita glimpses a bright red, ragged wrist scar as it disappears into his sleeve. Vijov glances up, and she feels a jolt in her bones.

"I worry," she says, stumbling back. "I worry about Quilla."

"Don't," he says. It's more an order than a reassurance.

She leaves his check on the counter and makes her rounds, refilling coffee cups and water glasses. When she goes back to him, he shoves his cup away, tosses a rumpled dollar on the check, and stalks out.

An hour later, when Rita gets around to spindling his check, she sees on the back printed in block letters: "You swallow your disgust."

"He is so insane," Quilla whispers as Rita slides into the seat across from her.

Quilla looks gaunt now. Jeans and a long-sleeved shirt hang

loosely from her coat-hanger frame. Her cheeks are sunken, her eyes dark, her complexion pale as biscuit dough. Her earrings are copper leaves—gingko leaves—dangling from wire hooks. Her cracked lips are the color of cherries. Her pulse shows, blue in the hollow of her neck, a birdlike throbbing beneath tissue-paper skin.

"Listen, honey," Rita says. "We need to get you to a doctor."

"I couldn't." Her voice is coarse, a pained rasp. "Georgi doesn't believe in those who claim healing powers. They mess with your essence, screw with your fate. You end up with someone else's blood in your veins, living someone else's life."

"He was here yesterday," Rita says. "He told you?"

"He tunneled into your emotions. What he found caused him great pain." Quilla's eyes glisten. "Georgi isn't easy to comprehend. I know. I was like you not long ago."

"It's not my way to interfere," Rita says. She knows that's just what she's doing, though. "But if he's insane like you say, why stay?"

"Oh no." Quilla's says. "Not that kind of insane. Georgi is a genius. His insanity is the kind you only find in great artists."

"I worry," Rita says. "Isn't there something I can do?"

"I'm okay." She fingers a lock of dull hair that's fallen across her forehead, twists it. "Really."

"I saw the scar on his wrist."

"He has others," Quilla says. "It's not what you think though. He wouldn't end his own life. Never."

"Why the scars then?"

"To transcend this sphere, to free himself from earthly restrictions, he confronts its limits and taboos. He demonstrates to the cosmos and to himself that these things hold no power over him."

"So he cuts his wrists?"

"To show that he can," she says. "Not to die."

"He could," Rita says. "Die."

"As long as he's afraid to possess his own body," Quilla says, "to cut it, to pierce it, to put emblems of his own creation on the skin, until he does that, he lives in the body his parents made. It cannot truly be his." Quilla hasn't touched her tea, but she's emptied her water glass. Now she's chewing the ice.

Rita shows her Vijov's diner check, the note he wrote there.

Quilla steadies it with her hand and reads. "He acknowledges your disgust. He purges himself of it, frees himself."

"He's crazy."

"I like you, Rita." Quilla's gaze goes past her. "That grants you power over me."

"I like you too," Rita says. A shudder runs up her back, and she wonders now why Quilla came. "You're just confused."

"I won't be back," Quilla says, and she slides out of the booth. "Your affection holds a power over me, influences me."

"Honey," Rita says, "the only influence you should get rid of is Georgi Vijov."

"He said you'd say that." Her voice is soft as sand. "It's worth it, Rita, worth everything. We'll be okay."

Quilla's hands come up, and they take Rita's face. There is a fluttery sound in Quilla's throat as she brushes air-kisses across each cheek. Quilla's fragrance is as sweet as burley blooms. Rita feels a whisper-breeze as gingko leaves brush her cheek and neck. An ache like a cave grows inside. She kisses Quilla's cheek, her hairline, and then her cherry red lips. She's never kissed a woman like this before, never thought to. Yet she kisses Quilla now, kisses her lips like a lover's.

Quilla pulls free. "You shouldn't," she whispers. There's a startled look in her eyes.

Rita's heart is a hammer in her chest. "You can come back," she tells Quilla. "Come back anytime."

Maybe Quilla will remember this moment. Rita wants that desperately. Maybe her friend, so brave now, will remember when this thing with Vijov unravels. Surely it will. Maybe her friend will remember, Rita tells herself as she grabs her rag from the counter, when she comes face-to-face with her own kind of regret.

Rose

For weeks after your hospital stay, I brought you roses, a dozen each morning. Online you bought me an inflatable lady, named her "Rose" —your delightful, sick-wife humor.

You unfurled Rose's vinyl skin, uncapped the plastic tube tucked into her back, and slipped it between your pallid lips. How long did you take, inflating her, pausing breathlessly, yet refusing help?

You're gone now. It's been one long, hollow year.

I find Rose in our closet. She's saggy and sad. I uncap her plastic tube and pull her close. On my cheek, my neck, I feel again your whisper-soft breath.

Birds of Providence

Sometimes Denton Weeks would park across from Alyssa's apartment building, the twelve-story balconied box she moved to when they broke up. Through the windshield, he'd watch as people whooshed in and out of the lobby door. Slumped behind the steering wheel, he'd remember those few weeks when he and Alyssa—housemates, coworkers, and rising stars at Coughlin Securities—had been lovers too.

He'd recall her sly smile, how her laughter would erupt, how her scent lingered on the pillow long after she'd left the bed. And when he'd overdosed on remembered love, when he felt completely pathetic, he'd slip his favorite Steve Earle disk into the car's CD player. He'd kick up the volume, hold on, and let the music rescue him.

Dent lived in a two-story house on Water Street in Providence. He and housemate Gabrielle Moreau shared the place, shared it first with Alyssa and later with a man named Victor Rosario.

Victor was tall and disarmingly affable. His gaze felt too penetrating though. His very presence seemed foreign at times and slightly invasive. Victor's cell phone rang with a warbling trill, an electronic version of the twelve-note mating call of the male indigo bunting. At first Dent liked the ring's flighty exuberance. It reminded him of the outdoors, of the Kentucky hills where he'd grown up, of the birds that sang so exuberantly, as if witnessing their first sunrise, as if they'd never seen spring before.

Victor's phone rang often, though, sometimes late at night. Before long, it began to irritate Dent. "How," he finally asked, "do female buntings stand a full season of that?"

The calls often involved Victor's work, a crisis of some sort, an African crane acting strangely, an owl on the ground, penguins huddled in their house. He was staff ornithologist at Roger Williams Park Zoo, a part-time position. He refused to look for work outside his profession. It was a matter of pride, Gabby said. Instead, Victor bought business cards with bright Audubon prints and sought freelance work.

Work was scarce, though, for a freelance ornithologist. Occasionally a seagull crashed into someone's oceanfront window, wrens nested in a Newport portico, or a birder reported spotting some extinct woodpecker in a Swansea birch grove. But most days Victor ended up working in the yard, pruning, weeding, or transplanting.

Many cellular bunting trills weren't about Victor's work though. They were from women he'd met in local nightclubs. Victor always seemed to connect. The women who called, those Dent had met, were no late-night consolation prizes either. They were attractive and smart. Dent wouldn't rank them in Alyssa's class, but they came close.

One Tuesday in October, Gabby's black bean lasagna bubbled in the oven. Its glorious scent filled the house. At the kitchen island, she snipped cilantro leaves, sprinkling the bits over the Romano tomato slices she had spread on a plate. As she worked, she hummed. It occurred to Dent, emptying the dishwasher, that he envied Gabby and her easy bliss.

A strange cell phone ring came from the front room—the drum riff from the Scissor Sisters' "I Don't Feel Like Dancin'." Victor muted the TV and answered. A minute later he strolled into the kitchen.

"What was that?" Gabby asked.

Victor opened the refrigerator door and peered in. "Alyssa," he said. The name hit Dent like a gut punch.

"No," Gabby said, oblivious. "That new cell ring."

Victor's face brightened. "Scissor Sisters. You like it?"

"I do," Gabby said. She danced past him, nine-inch Henckel blade in hand. From the crisper drawer she grabbed a carton of shitake mushrooms. She slit the cover and dumped them on her cutting board. "What happened to your bunting song?"

"It got confusing, working in the yard," he said. "You know that mockingbird nesting out front? It mimics the ring now."

For months after Alyssa moved out, Dent left her room vacant. "Maybe she'll change her mind," he told Gabby. But in July he started a new job, this one with Washington Trust. He decided then it was time to place the ad for another housemate.

The first afternoon Gabby took three calls. "This one sounds nice," she said, pointing at the pad with her pencil. "Cuban, maybe?" She circled a number and name—Victor Rosario. "A biologist or zoologist or something." She flipped the pad over and looked at Dent. "Unless you want another woman in that room."

That was the last thing he wanted. "You won't feel outnumbered?"

Gabby said, "Maybe I'll get some appreciation." She'd had issues with Alyssa, imagined slights, a seeming lack of respect, all of it happening at female frequencies well beyond Dent's perception range.

"You interview the guy, then," he told Gabby. "Size this Victor up. See how he fits in our little family."

Gabby Moreau, three years younger than Denton Weeks, was round-faced and full-cheeked, yet surprisingly trim, considering her passion for food. She smiled often, and when she did, her eyes squinted in a pixyish way. A former Navy cook, she studied culinary arts now at Johnson and Wales.

Gabby loved cooking, loved it seemingly to the exclusion of all else. When not actually cooking, she'd watch others cook, Rachael Ray or Nigella Lawson, shows she'd TiVo and replay. She read cookbooks and collected them, stacks of cookbooks, popular and obscure, domestic cuisine and foreign. She loved kitchen tools too—the Henckel knives, bright plastic yolk separators, radish rosetters, slaw shredders, stainless steel mixing bowls, and wooden-handled whisks. She lusted for the newest Cuisinart, the brushed stainless model with a smoked-glass lid. Dent knew of no love interest in Gabby's life, male or female. Only food.

Dent phoned the number Gabby had circled on the phone pad. Fifteen minutes later, Victor Rosario knocked on the door, his copy of the newspaper with Dent's housemate ad folded under his arm. He extended a business card. Dent glanced at it, slipped it into a pocket.

Despite Victor's height—he was several inches taller than Dent —he seemed to glide striding across the hardwood floor. Dent showed him the downstairs, the kitchen, and the enclosed back porch, which doubled as an exercise room. Victor seemed to take it all in.

Upstairs, Dent pushed open the door to Alyssa's old room. He could sense her there still, some small essence she hadn't been able to pack up and cart away. The room echoed, the wall hooks missing her Kandinsky prints, the bare mattress, the abandoned desk and stuffed chair, the wire hangers dangling oddly from a closet rod, and above them a length of sea-blue shelf paper pushed up in a wave.

As Victor paused in the doorway, the joints of his lanky body seemed to click into new, latched positions. His fingers followed the contours of the door molding up to the lintel, studying it as a blind man's would.

"It's old," Victor said. "This room, it has history, character. I like it." He'd want to repaint, he said, walls and ceiling both. He'd strip the door casing too, the ornate baseboard, and the cornice bordering the room, strip them to the wood beneath.

At the kitchen table, Victor wrote a deposit check.

"I cook," Gabby said, claiming her territory. "It's what I do."

Dent told him about parking, how to get three cars off the street each evening, about morning shower schedules, about shared bills, household chores, and privacy.

Later that night, Dent found Victor's business card. He held it near the lamp and studied the bird painting there. Off its limb, the bird's body looked contorted. Its feathers—black, tan, and white—spread out like fingers on a hand. It had startled eyes, and it seemed to flail in some middle space between nest and flight.

Victor dabbed more stripping gel onto his sponge. "How long have you worked there," he asked, "for this Washington Trust?"

"Two months." Dent looked up from his work on the baseboard, refolded his gel-soaked rag. A window fan blew fumes from the room. Still, his throat burned, his eyes watered.

"And before that?" Victor asked.

"Coughlin Securities. Senior Account Manager." Dent always liked the sound of that. He picked up the can of stripping solution and read the label. "This stuff toxic?"

"My Uncle Nestor, he uses it many times to strip boats." Victor wiped his brow with the back of his wrist. "You did not want to leave your old job?"

"Gabby tell you that?"

"It is on your face when you speak of it."

Dent told Victor the story then. He tried to tell it dispassionately, as if the job, the woman, the sorry way everything ended, as if all this had happened to some other hapless soul.

He'd met Alyssa seven years ago. They were summer interns at Coughlin Securities, he a carefree senior at the University of Kentucky, she this brilliant junior from UMass. Dent joined the firm after graduating, and she joined a year later. At first, theirs was a business partnership—late nights developing parametric stock screens, weekends coauthoring research reports. They made a great pair, with her analysis and his more intuitive insights. They were written up in *Business Daily,* gave opinions on CNBC, always the two of them together.

Dent dated other women sporadically, none special. They would recognize him from TV, tell him he looked slimmer in person. They liked his accent, which he'd tried to lose and thought he had. Apparently not. Meanwhile, Alyssa alternately lived with and broke up with Johnny Oh, the wiry, ponytailed director of the Providence Art League. The splits were brief, tumultuous. Dent kept a room open for her in the house on Water Street, a retreat of sorts when things became too furious.

"Why she kept going back to Oh, I never figured out," Dent told Victor. "He wasn't worthy of her." He felt somehow disloyal, felt exposed, spilling all this. Victor was so disarming though, insinuating, and once Dent started, he didn't stop.

Whenever former Coughlin comrades gathered at Dorrence Pub, conversation would turn to Alyssa Larkin. Denton Weeks would join in trashing her. He'd mimic her gestures, imitate her way of speaking, her clipped words. It was something he'd always been good at. Yet now here he was listing Alyssa's better points to his new housemate, Victor Rosario, this vaguely foreign man he hardly knew.

Blame the fumes, he thought, the turpentine.

Victor set his wood-stripping tools aside and went to the kitchen. He came back with a bottle of Hatuey Cuban beer and two glasses. He handed one to Dent and poured. "This Alyssa, she was never your lover?"

Dent drank. The beer tasted woodsy on his tongue, mellow going down. He looked up, regarded the man. "Eleven weeks," he said finally. "When Alyssa quit Johnny Oh for good, she landed with me. Easiest rebound ever. Trouble is, it had nothing to do with me." A sad laugh escaped. He put the bottle down and wiped his hands on his jeans.

"Nothing?" Victor turned the bottle in his hands. He chiseled with a thumbnail at a corner of the red and gold label.

"I was here." Dent shrugged. "Convenient. I don't know." He

went to the window and looked out. The fan's breeze flapped his shirttail. "Anyway, this Boston honcho, Max Chambers, he flies in one Monday, comes roaring through the office like this damn chain saw, downsizing us. Heads roll—good people, including the guy who manages the place. Chambers installs Alyssa on that perch, tells me and the other six survivors that we now report to her."

"Ah," Victor said. "This is difficult for your romance."

"I didn't care," Dent said. "Alyssa said it'd never work though. She wouldn't even try, just packed her stuff and moved out." He returned to the place on the baseboard where he'd left off. "You know what really hurt? She made this grand prediction like she knows my future. 'Someday you'll see I'm right,' she tells me, 'once you get some distance.'"

"So your job is lost because of this, your pride, your honor?"

"Worse. I hang around for months, hoping things will change, which they don't. Then, when the job market's totally tanked, I march into Alyssa's new office, and I hand her my resignation! How weak is that?"

"Very weak," Victor said.

"She tries to talk me out of it, says she needs me there. But by that time I'd gone all in. There was no backing out." Dent picked up his rag and began wiping stripper solution onto the baseboard again. "I thought it'd make a difference, me working somewhere else. We'd be untangled, and Alyssa would move back here."

Victor lifted his glass as if making a toast. "With women, there is not so much difference between the gallant and the foolish."

Dent raised his glass but set it down without drinking. "You know how it gets right after a concert? You're still juiced, but the band's gone, the lights come up, and there's this moment you're confused, because you've still got this great show playing in your head, but now your crappy world's come back?"

"Si," Victor said.

"That's how it felt getting flushed." He reached for the can again. There was a stinging in his eyes, but he didn't stop to wipe them, and he didn't look up.

On that October evening, as the aroma of black bean lasagna filled the Water Street house, as Gabby chopped shitakes, as the word "Alyssa," still fresh from Victor's lips, hung there in the kitchen, Dent snatched up his car keys and rushed out the door.

Alyssa. Alyssa. Her name was a hiss in his brain.

Behind him, the screen door slammed. Victor yelled something about not being stupid. Dent had no idea what Victor thought was stupid. He didn't care. He'd had his fill of Victor's slick act. Things were screwed up with Alyssa. Worse yet, *he'd* screwed them up. He'd thought she'd feel beholden to him. All this time he'd been waiting for her, waiting for something to change, living life while barely letting himself breathe.

Dent parked across from her apartment building, as he'd done so often before. This time he got out though. He crossed the street and pushed through the lobby door. A security guard looked up from inside his chicken-wire cage.

"Alyssa Larkin," Dent said.

"You expected?" The guard jerked a microphone nearer his mouth.

"Tell her it's Denton Weeks."

The guard hesitated. Then he tapped a keyboard and spoke Dent's name. An ocean sound gushed from a speaker, with it Alyssa's voice. "It's okay, Arthur. Send him up."

The guard's finger poked a button. A bell dinged. Elevator doors slid open.

Dent crossed the lobby and stepped into the elevator. How many times, he wondered, had she ridden this elevator, stood in this exact place?

As the doors closed, Dent thrust his hand into their rubber guillotine. The doors bounced and opened again. "What's her apartment number?" he called across the lobby.

An annoyed look, a small shake of his head. "Four-oh-seven."

Dent pushed the button for four.

The elevator stopped, but Denton Weeks's stomach didn't, not until it lodged somewhere between his lungs. He stumbled into the hall. Small light fixtures, fake candles with dim amber bulbs, spread vague puddles of light down the maroon carpet. A disinfectant smell made Dent's skin tingle. He started down the hall, veered right, and saw her.

Alyssa Larkin leaned out from her apartment doorway. Her Patriot football jersey ended midthigh. Her hair was wrapped in a turban towel, the kind that kept it dry, more or less, during quick showers. "Caught me in the shower," she said. "I was just going out."

"A date?"

"Hardly," she said. "Chambers is down from Boston." She made a face as if swallowing medicine.

Chambers was a small man, brilliant with numbers. No sense of humor inside his shaved head though, no warmth behind his reptilian eyes. An image flashed through Dent's mind—Alyssa and Chambers in bed, sheets tangled, twisted to ropes. Just as suddenly, mercifully, it faded.

Alyssa backed into her apartment. Her gaze on Dent's chest seemed to steady him and tug him in. She closed the door. "Mix yourself a drink while I get ready." She disappeared through a beaded curtain into another room.

Her apartment was smaller than he'd imagined. Her furniture looked awkward in this room. She'd hung her framed Kandinsky prints, but they seemed misplaced against the faux-thatch wallpaper. Dent walked to the balcony door and looked across the narrow concrete platform and wall. Her apartment view was a rising hillside of drab three-decker houses. She lived on the wrong side of the building for the coveted river view. Dent felt a pleasant glow, a kind of sunrise inside. He turned back to the room, and when he did, he spotted Victor Rosario's business card. It was there on her coffee table, blatant and brilliant in its full Audubon plumage.

He picked up the card, put it down. "Victor Rosario is my housemate," he called through the beads. "Did you know?"

"So he said." No hesitation. No surprise.

Dent opened the refrigerator. Beer—six bottles of Hatuey Cuban right up front, her Bud Light behind. A jug of mango juice too, Alyssa's morning favorite. Styrofoam cartons of leftover takeout—Chinese, Greek, Thai. Diet Coke. Cheeses—Muenster, Gruyère, and Gorgonzola. *Some things never change.*

He found a glass, dropped in ice, mixed gin and tonic. "Can I fix you a drink?"

"I wish," she called from the other room. "No. I'll need my wits tonight. Chambers is a shark."

The name irritated Dent. He couldn't help it. "A bald-headed varmint," he muttered.

"It's serious," she said, coming back through the beads. "There's blood in the water, you know."

Dent stirred his ice with a finger and sipped. "Sounds rough."

Alyssa padded toward him, her feet bare. She wore a bright blue dress now, blue like a jewel. Indigo, maybe. Dent couldn't be sure. Her hair had an odd lump on one side, as if she'd just gotten up from a nap. With both hands she worked to unsnarl a pantyhose wad. "Tell me I don't look awful, Dent," she said. "Lie if you have to, but tell me, please?"

"You look great," he said. He almost meant it.

She sat and jabbed a foot into the hose.

"You and Victor," he asked, "how'd that happen?"

She shrugged. "We just met."

"You knew he was my housemate?"

When she got her other leg started, she stood and tugged the pantyhose up, squatted into them, plucked them straight. "What's it matter?" Alyssa asked. "We've got history, you and me. That doesn't give you rights."

"Of all the men on Earth—"

"Victor's nice. I like him. We have fun. So what?"

Dent fingered his glass. "It hurts," he said. "That's all."

She moved closer and turned. "Do me?" She meant her dress, the zipper and hook.

He gave her the drink to hold. She sipped. He tugged, but the zipper slide was stuck. "Suck in," he said. He tugged again, and the slide ran to the top. Alyssa's warm, familiar scent came up to him, and he breathed it in. She held her hair aside, and he hooked the snap at the nape of her neck. He resisted an urge to seal it there with his lips.

Dent's fingers touched her neck hairs, fine as feathers and curled down. Dry, too. No turban towel could have kept them that dry, not if she'd really just come from the shower. He backed away, made wary by her lie. Excited by it too.

"Listen," Alyssa said, turning to face him again. "Victor's sweet. Let's leave it there." She handed back his glass. "I've got bigger problems. You're smart about this stuff. Why do you think Chambers is in town?"

He tried to pat her hair lump flat. "For the lobster?"

She swatted at him, missed. "I'm serious, Dent."

Alyssa's hands went to Dent's chest. "I'll tell you why Chambers is here," she said. "Commissions are down twelve percent. Our institutional portfolio is a serious underperformer." She seemed flustered, unusual for Alyssa. And she wanted something from him.

"So," he said, not knowing what, "Chambers."

Her gaze dropped to her hands. "I could get your job back, Dent. I could. Same job." She leaned close again. "Chambers is desperate for answers, for solutions. I can broach the subject tonight, maybe get you a raise."

"Twenty percent?" Dent answered with a speed that startled him.

She started to turn away. "I don't make that much."

"What then? You tell me," he said. "Twelve percent? Fifteen?"

"I'll do what I can," she said, coming back. "Chambers is no fool."

Dent could feel his power now, a heady thing, something he hadn't felt in a very long while. "And Victor. What about him?"

"Why keep bringing up Victor?" Red splotches bloomed on her neck, her anger rash. She went to the bedroom and returned with flat shoes in her hand. "I need to know, Dent. Chambers will be here soon. Tell me. Do I let him know you can be had?"

In his ears, Dent heard the whoosh of his pulse. He finished the drink, swirled the ice, savored the fading taste, savored the moment. At the refrigerator, he refilled the glass, this time with mango juice. He drank, and he remembered then how he'd liked it too.

Alyssa limped into the kitchen, a shoe on her right foot, carrying the other. "Okay," she said. "You win." She balanced herself with a hand on the counter and slid her foot into the second shoe. "Let's say things go well with Chambers tonight. And let's say I get you some kind of raise. Maybe ten percent. I'll ask for the enchilada."

"Say you do."

"Here's the deal. You'll have charge of the institutional portfolio. Free rein."

"And Victor?"

Alyssa grimaced. "Damn it, Dent! Let it go!" She straightened her dress, the sleeves and bodice. She looked good. She always looked good in that shade of blue.

"I can't do this alone," she said. "You and me, we're good together. Remember?"

"And Victor?" he said again.

Inside that dress, Alyssa seemed to deflate. "And Victor . . . is history."

Dent went to her, touched her lips, her cheek. "You'd do that?"

"You're telling me that's what it takes?"

Victor was sitting on the front steps, his cell phone wedged between shoulder and ear, when Dent got home. It seemed that someone's parakeet had sneezed, fallen to the floor of its cage, and refused to climb back onto its perch.

Dent leaned against the cold iron railing, waiting. A hint of first frost was in the air, a cold tickle in his nose. The mockingbird, sitting atop the dark pine, practiced a new tune. On the phone, Victor prescribed sugar water for the parakeet and twelve hours in a darkened cage. He flipped the phone shut and slid it into a pocket. "You went to Alyssa?"

Dent told him what she'd said, the part about his old job. He skipped the part about Victor being history. He'd leave that for her.

"I did not think you wanted this job again," Victor said.

"Working with Alyssa? *Sí*," Dent said. "She's special. But you know that."

"Not so special, *compañero*." Victor's hand fluttered up toward the streetlight. "But this is personal, a question of taste."

Dent said, "You've been seeing her."

"Seeing her?" Victor's gaze was on him now, watching. "*Sí*," Victor said at last. "Last night, the upstairs bar at Dorrence Pub. She introduces herself. We exchange cards. At first I do not see that this is your Alyssa."

"Last night?"

Victor stood to go inside. "She sees I drink Hatuey and buys me another," he said. "Very aggressive, this woman, who talks only of herself. I leave her card on the bar so she will know I have no interest."

Dent jammed his hands into his pockets. For several minutes after Victor had left, he looked out toward the streetlight, watching his breath rise like pale clouds and disappear in the chill evening air. Then he went inside too. There was a garlic and butter smell in the air. A sizzling sound came from the kitchen, and Gabby hummed another unrecognizable song.

Dent rummaged through stacked music disks, scattered newspapers and plastic cases across the dark hardwood floor. He found his Steve Earle rip, loaded it, and killed the room lights. He stretched out on the floor, newspapers everywhere, and with fingers pressing the earbuds in deep, tried to shut out everything but his tunes.

The Persistence of Ice

February 4, 2008

Mr. Lisle Titsworth Sr.
Room 412, St. Francis Extended Care Facility
1135 Charles Blvd.
Louisville KY 40213

Dear Father,

Shortly I will explain why you receive a letter from your loving son written in unfamiliar hand, this in lieu of my customary Saturday visit. Surely you noticed that I was not there this past week or the prior one. The reasons stem from a situation that has developed with a student in recent weeks, a situation which, in the beginning, I thought quite trivial. In light of your current state of health, I thought it best that I try to manage the situation without benefit of your wise counsel.

I trust that some kind nurse or volunteer reads this letter to you. She must know that she has my most sincere appreciation. I remain confident that, given the kind ministrations of the St. Francis staff, your iron will and lion heart shall soon prevail against the forces besieging you.

The six-month report from Doctor Watts arrived yesterday. In

it he writes that your cognitive functions are almost completely restored. Alas, some motor skills may never return. Still, it seems that
you are more fortunate than most who experience such strokes. I
asked specifically, and he assures me that you retain the ability to
read. Thus you may explore the world once more in the company of
your beloved Dickens, Kipling, and Durant.

He also reports that your malaise inexplicably remains. You
only need summon your most formidable resources of will, Father,
and throw off that dark shroud. I remain confident that you shall
one day do just that.

Now if you will indulge me, I shall relate the rather improbable
circumstances to which I alluded above.

You may recall that it was requested by the Burkitt County
Board of Education that I conduct a basic civics course this school
year, a mandatory one. Their aim was to inculcate the bare essentials
of societal norms into those who are about to complete their education and spew forth into the world. I submitted a skeletal version of
Lessons of History, the course I have taught, in one form or another,
to students in St. Louis, Urbana, and Clear Lake over my twenty-
two-year career. Quite naturally, it was approved.

Is it possible that you ever encountered students of the ilk con-
fronting me that first day? Perhaps, but it would truly amaze me.
Such students I had seen in hallways, but my courses tend to attract
few heathens such as these. Quite frankly, I had grown accustomed
to classes filled with minds which, if not eager to learn, were at least
resigned to the need to exert a modicum of effort in that direction.
By slovenly posture, gross inattention, and jokes of the most objec-
tionable kind, these students exhibit a total disregard not only for
me but also for the material being presented. Of course, I was not
totally unprepared, defenseless as I stood before this unwashed
horde. You, having toiled yourself in the classroom for so many
years, have taught me well. Rest assured that I employed every verbal
trick you have taught me. Rapier wit, deft sarcasm, every means at
my disposal was deployed to right this situation.

One youth in particular, his name Drew Prewitt, a rotund young man who quite uncharacteristically moves with a dancer's grace, seemed to command an inordinate proportion of the class's attention.

How many students have reveled in the muffled snickers of their classmates who address me by the name we share, you and I? Hundreds? At a minimum. Each fall, adolescents discover anew the humor in pronouncing "Titsworth" aloud in public. Young Mr. Prewitt took particular pleasure in this, addressing me by name to end his every sentence. With each question, his hand would shoot up, and when called upon, he would embark upon a rambling monologue having little or no bearing on the particular question posed. His protracted prattle served only as filler between untold repetitions of my name, with variably misapplied emphasis for heightened comedic effect. This penchant did not dwindle after a week or two, as is the norm. By mid-October, I was preparing to invite young Mr. Prewitt to a private conference at which I would spell out how I had handled similar situations in the past, in order that he might understand the full consequences should he persist in this sophomoric nonsense. Fortunately for him, his abuse of our name ended quite suddenly on its own.

Unfortunately, young Puck did not cease his exaggerated level of class participation. To the contrary, if anything it increased. The others quite eagerly allowed him to bear all burdens of participation. While his answers now lacked the gratuitous use of my name, and while they took on what seemed to me a somewhat more learned tone, they still retained the meandering, dissociated quality typical of a non sequiter. This I found most disconcerting. Still, truth be told, several times young Mr. Prewitt happened upon reasonably defensible anarchist viewpoints in the course of his verbal ramblings.

Except for an occasional offering by Miss Gee, a young lady cursed with a misproportioned body and a caterwauling voice, young Prewitt was, for all intents and purposes, the only student offering

answers. I soon sensed that something else might be afoot, this con-
clusion based on sputtered laughter and muffled giggles from classmates whenever the lad spoke. I could not, try as I might, discern a
correlation between the content of what he said and the class reac-
tions. But I was determined to find him out. Perhaps, I thought, it
is not his words but some small action. And so one day I brought my
pocket tape recorder from home and secreted it in a book bag upon
my desk. I called on him often but ignored his words, focusing instead on his movements. But no matter how closely I watched him—
watched his hands, his eyes, how his large and slovenly body moved
as he answered—I did not discern how the lad was managing to en-
tertain my class right beneath my very nose.

The answer surfaced that evening when I reviewed the tape
made in class. First I heard the sound of footsteps shuffling in, followed by a minute more of clatter—Miss Gee, who sits front row
center, kicking her shoes off and flipping them about with her
feet—as I began the day's lesson. I posed a question concerning
checks and balances, then called upon young Prewitt. His response
momentarily confused me. Strange to say, the lad spoke with your
voice, only younger, sounding as you did in my youth. But surely, I
thought, this is not possible. Still, without the visual distraction of
his hefty physicality and kinetic energy, the voice was unmistakable.
Then I responded on the tape, and I knew. It was not you whom the
lad mimicked. It was I.

Would you be relieved to know that, despite his provocation, I
did not resort to the tactics that I previously employed in Clear
Lake? Perhaps so.

The next morning I waited with recorder and tape outside
Principal Yates's office. You may recall my telling you about Yates, a
true toady to the school board. The man is a most unfortunate
blending of soft disciplinarian and ineffectual administrator. Still,
I thought it best to seek redress through proper channels this time.

Suffice it to say, his response was most disappointing. As he
listened to the tape, it seemed unequivocal. The lad mimicked me.

Yet when I reached to shut the recorder off, he requested that I allow the tape to play through to the very end. As God is my witness, a smile broke across his face at one point, and he quickly turned toward the office window.

That afternoon, the loudspeakers summoned Drew Prewitt to Principal Yates's office. The following morning a handwritten note offered his apology for any embarrassment or chagrin that may have been occasioned by the prank. I went promptly to Yates's office, where I voiced my outrage at the note's mocking and sycophantic tone. Predictably, no further action was taken.

Understandably, I had lost all confidence in the weak administrators of this school. I would no longer subject myself to this humiliation. It became of no consequence that the course outline prescribed a minimum of fifty percent classroom discussion. I would no longer provide the stage upon which Mr. Prewitt danced his merry jig. I would lecture for the full hour every day. Naturally, this required that I prepare new material each evening. But I know this material well, and the marginal effort proved to be quite inconsequential. Truth be told, I relished the prospect of reasserting control of my classroom.

I do not contend that my lectures were invariably brilliant. I do not contend that all students learned. But I do contend that any subsequent failure to learn cannot be attributed to incomplete or ineffective presentation on my part. Many students chose to nap. Some chose to engage in unrelated activities. I maintained a laissez-faire policy toward them, provided they did not disturb those who showed even slight interest. By my count, listeners initially totaled perhaps ten of the thirty-three. Among them were Miss Gee and, surprisingly, young Mr. Prewitt. In fact, as Christmas break approached, my lectures began to attract a few more listeners. Pencils occasionally jotted in notebooks now, and I felt certain that they were at last responding to lecture points well made. I could sense their surging interest. In response, I increased the time spent each night on lectures for the basic class, often appropriating time from

preparation for my college-bound students, as I sought more effec-
tive ways to present the material and augment my primary lecture
points.

Had I somehow happened upon the key to holding their flighty
attentions? Perhaps so. Despite our rocky beginnings, I must con-
fess that I felt more than slight gratification at this fortuitous turn of
events.

Reality dashed my small pedagogic victory shortly after the
holidays. I must have harbored niggling suspicions throughout the
seemingly miraculous renaissance. Looking back, I see that the evidence was there. Quiz scores did not improve. No one, save the annoying Miss Gee, approached me outside class with questions or
requests for help. Perhaps most telling, though, were inexplicable
outbursts of enthusiasm and clandestine celebrations, often at the
most inconsequential points of my lecture. Something was amiss.
Still, I dismissed the early signs, preferring the illusion that I was
teaching and my students were learning.

That illusion died one snowy January morning. A teary Miss
Gee met me in the faculty parking lot. Between bosom-bobbing
sobs, she screeched out her tale of woe. It seems that she had been
taunted by several young men, over what it was not clear. I suggested
that Principal Yates was better equipped to handle such complaints.
She understood, she sobbed. But there was something she wanted
me to know. Check out the wall, she said. Back side, high on the
right.

This I must explain. There is an edifice beyond the playing
fields here at Burkitt County High School, a cinder-block construction of peculiar shape. It serves no discernible function save this—it
is layered with the most vile graffiti, or so I am told. I am unsure of
the wall's origin, but suffice it to say it is solely the students' domain.
By tradition, we faculty steer clear. For unfathomable reasons, our
lax administration permits this affront to all civility to stand on
school property.

Second period was open on my schedule, so I bundled up in

boots and gloves and trekked out to the wall. I averted my gaze from what is scribbled there, reading nothing as I circled round to the back side. There I focused my attention high up on the right.

We all develop, through the years, certain mannerisms, certain ways of speaking, certain phrases that we favor in our normal speech. In this I am no different from you or others. Such propensities in phrasing are most natural. But apparently my basic civics students found something entertaining in my phraseology. Apparently, I say, because they had posted a tote board of sorts, not unlike that used for betting on sporting events. Perhaps a dozen students had penciled their names in as contestants. Each was assigned, or more likely had chosen, a specific phrase. Drew Prewitt, for example, had selected "perhaps so." A long string of tick marks suggested that young Prewitt had chosen well.

You were a teacher, Father, so I trust you understand. I had been duped once more, not by our college-bound elite but quite frankly by our dregs. All teachers know that frightening but wondrous, albeit rare, moment when they are surpassed by truly exceptional pupils. But these are not those students. I daresay none will surpass me at any point in life. Yet they treat me and my subject matter with gleeful disregard. Surely you understand my resultant rage.

In hindsight, perhaps I was naive in thinking that the administration might now take decisive action. I supplied them evidence in the form of instant photographs that very day. I submitted my recommendations in writing at Wednesday's board meeting. My demands were simple and quite justified: Level the wall, suspend Prewitt for the balance of the semester, and suspend each of the other participants for two weeks. In my verbal presentation, I stated quite clearly that I would abide no compromise. The time has come, I implored, to stop coddling these juveniles.

The board retreated to a closed session, returning in scant minutes to render a decision that should not have surprised me. They opted for a weak compromise. Young Prewitt was suspended for five days. Five days! The others received but light detention. The wall would remain untouched.

There is a certain justice awaiting these young men. This I know. At graduation, they will face the world outside. How quickly they will sink into a proletarian existence, condemned to live out their lives in mind-numbing mediocrity. I see a sad justice in their fate.

But the wall is yet another matter. While students come and go and eventually, for good or ill, meet their just deserts, that wall is allowed to stand from year to year. It is never called to a just accounting. Until now, that is.

In Clear Lake I foolishly utilized plastic pipe for my explosive, a choice based solely on price. You may recall my telling how the device split quite harmlessly, how it fizzled when discharged into the office of my nemesis there, sounding to all the world like one elongated fart. (You will excuse my vulgarity, Father. There is no more accurate description for that seemingly endless expelling of wretchedly sulfurous fumes.)

I would not repeat that error.

That very afternoon I purchased a short length of pipe—this time galvanized, three-quarter inch—and three boxes of stove matches. After snipping the match heads off with nail clippers, I packed them, with all due caution, into the pipe. Then I capped and sealed the ends.

Their wall would soon fall

At dusk, I pocketed my device, donned a wool parka, scarf, and gloves, and headed out into the snowy night. Little traffic was about. I am certain that I was unseen as I made my way in snow that had accumulated by then to perhaps ten inches. Walking, I could feel the pipe rub, heavy against my leg. I felt that glorious surge of righteous energy, and my pace quickened. I stumbled on an unseen step at the entrance to the playing fields. In the instant that I fell, hands out, face down in the snow, I wondered if my device might detonate, if it might disembowel me, or worse, where I fell.

Needless to report, it did not.

Snow had worked its way under my scarf. My slacks and parka were coated. I brushed myself off as best I could, my gloves themselves now snow-crusted. I checked my payload. It still nestled warm against me.

The experience of falling suggested that I might more prudently transport the device pressed not so close to my body. So the remainder of the way, it rested in my gloved hand. Were I to fall, I would quickly toss it some distance away.

But I did not fall again. I pushed my way through frigid wind and blowing snow, eventually arriving, quite exhausted, at the wall.

The edifice looked larger than I remembered, as I stood regarding it that snowy evening. I wondered if my device would bring the entire structure down or if it might only damage part. For a moment, I toyed with the idea of retreating to my apartment to construct a second, larger weapon. No, I decided. This one would do. Damaged or destroyed, either was preferable to what stood before me now.

I selected the spot where the pipe should strike the wall—back side toward the right. I stepped off twenty paces, a distance that seemed quite safe, and yet one at which the device could be hurled against the wall with sufficient force to explode.

You may recall that, following the dud at Clear Lake, you commented quite wittily that I would have been well served by more thorough studies in the physical sciences. Father, I fear your observation has held true yet again.

You have, no doubt, heard tales of children whose tongues stuck to school-yard flagpoles. I do not know if these are true, but I can now assure you that they are based on sound principles of science. Just as a frigid pipe can freeze spittle and attach to tongues, so will a pipe, in cooling, melt snow on a glove and attach to it.

When I threw the pipe, it traveled perhaps six feet, having extracted the glove from my throwing hand. Together, they burrowed into the snow.

Had I considered my actions, I would have reacted differently. Have no doubt of that. But reflex is not subject to rational review. I lurched forward to retrieve the device, as if my errant toss somehow did not count.

The pipe exploded in a brilliant, silent flash.

I say silent, but no doubt it was not. Suffice it to say that I recall no sound, only that moment of white flame. Partial deafness lingers yet today, evidencing the fact that indeed the detonation must have been accompanied by a mighty sound.

Lest you be overly concerned about my physical condition, Father, let me offer reassurance. Burns were limited to the exposed portions of my face. The nurse tells me that all traces of eyebrows are gone, imparting to me a visage of one perpetually surprised. My eyesight will, in all probability, be restored to a level that allows reading of large-print books. All major limbs are intact, and I am assured that most digits are salvageable.

Three people have visited me here in my recuperation bed, the first being the kindly volunteer who transcribes this letter. The second, Principal Yates, arrived this morning with paperwork in hand—the board's offer to provide a rather bland letter of recommendation, not unlike the one from Clear Lake, on the condition that I quietly resign. The only other visitor has been young Mr. Prewitt. Quite frankly, Father, I am at a loss, still, to fathom the lad.

I shall visit you again, I assure you, as soon as I am up and about. Until then, I remain,

Your loving son,
Lisle A. Titsworth Jr.

Shadow Flag

I feel strangely anonymous here in my old hometown. Untethered. Twenty-five years I've been gone, with just brief stopovers, which is what this one will have to be. Twenty-five years, and this town has forgotten John Fain. It might as well be forever.

I'm sitting at the counter of Rita's Huddle In Café, feeling reflective, nostalgic, poking my fork at what's left of a slice of Dutch apple pie. Rita topped it with cheddar and warmed it in the oven when I asked. Her gaze slid right over me though. Maybe she's busy. Or maybe she's forgotten the slim boy she kissed that summer long ago—kissed and so much more—deep in her uncle's tobacco field. Maybe it's the weight I carry now. Or maybe it's the mess that time has made of my face. I take a drink of sweet tea, set the sweating glass back on the soaked napkin, and ask myself what I'd expected.

"Someone here belong to an orange Corvette?" a kid asks from the doorway.

"That'd be me," I say.

My Ontario orange '72 Corvette Coupe, a decade-long garage project, always draws attention. She'll never be a show car. The engine, tranny, and chassis numbers don't match. Once the pros see that, they don't give her a second look. But she's sleek, she looks fast, and she can still turn heads. The staring usually makes me uncomfortable, so for months at a time, she stays in the garage. This time out I've enjoyed the attention though. I might as well. She'll be gone soon.

The Vette and I are on our farewell trip together. It's an odd blend of business and pleasure, of nostalgia and obligations. Our last stop will be Bowling Green and tomorrow's car convention. She'll go on the auction block there. With luck, she'll bring sixteen thousand, enough to cover my daughter Mandy's next tuition bill.

"Thought you'd want to know," the kid in the doorway says. "She's pissin' green in the gutter."

I drop money on the counter and head back into the day's building heat.

The car trickles coolant now, having already nearly emptied herself in the gutter. I pop the hood and pray it's just a busted hose. No such luck. The head gasket blew.

I ask the kid about a phone. He points me to the glass booth in front of United Bank, which I remember as Farmers First Bank. I drop a quarter in the slot, punch thirty-six numbers without once taking out my phone card, and wait for Carol, my wife, to answer. In the moment between the connecting click and first ring, it's the "Hello" of another Carol—my first wife, Carol—that I expect. She died of cancer seven years ago. I forget sometimes, my brain slipping years for a few seconds. But as the first ring fades, I know it will be Wife Carol Two answering, not Wife Carol One.

Outside, the bank clock flashes twelve minutes past noon, then 103 degrees. I'm broiling in this glass rotisserie.

Why am I calling anyway? This Carol doesn't need me to check in from the road, even if I am delayed. Not unless it affects her schedule, which this doesn't, not yet. As I go to hang up, I hear her pick up. "Carol Carver-Fain," she says.

I tell her about the car trouble.

"Where are you?" She asks. I tell her and hear an inrush of air between her teeth. "John," she says, "you said that was off your itinerary." She's right. Before I left, we sat down and prioritized tasks for this trip. There was more to be done than time allowed.

"It *is* off," I say. Seeing Randy, Monk, and Murlene, I mean. "I stopped here for lunch at a diner, that's all." We'd talked and decided that attending the Kirtchner with her on Sunday was more important than shooting pool with long-ago friends. I could find time for that next year.

"Car trouble?" she says. "How long will it take?"

"It's a gasket." I fish a handkerchief from my pocket.

"And how long is that?"

"Couple of hours," I tell her. I know better though. I'm not likely to find a replacement '72 Corvette 454 head gasket within twenty miles of here. Maybe not within a hundred miles.

"You know what Sunday means to me."

I do. Carol's art consumes her. She is on the verge of landing a prime slot in Kirtchner's fall exhibition. Press the right flesh on Sunday, she says, and the deal will be sealed. It's what she wants, and it's what I want for her.

"What's up, Dad?" says Bryan on the extension.

"Vette sprung a leak." I wipe my brow. The heat in the booth is stifling.

"You get the amp?"

"I haven't made it to Nashville yet."

"Warber's closes at six. They won't hold it."

"I'll try to get there, Bry. If not, we'll work something else out."

"Jeez, Dad. We're talking a vintage twelve-tube Drux Serenade Amp here. How many do you think there are?"

"Hundreds?" I answer. The heat is making me dizzy. I want my son to laugh like he used to. But it's Carol who laughs, and I want my smart answer back. Bryan is nineteen. He won't joke with me anymore, especially when this Carol is around.

"Screwed again," he mutters.

My son's favorite T-shirt is muddy brown with a puckered smiley face on the front. He wears it like defiance. The world is out to get Bryan Fain. He's convinced of that. Just ask, and he'll tick off a dozen instances to prove it. Now I've given him another one. The extension phone clicks—slammed, I imagine—and he's gone.

In the past three years, Bryan's life has turned from gold to gray. I don't know how to fix it. Community college wasn't the answer. Maybe this band of his will be. I'm no judge of talent, but when he talks about music, there's a hint of the old spark in him. That's why I said nothing when he shaved his head, when he and the others got neck tattoos. Part of the act—that's how I explained it to Carol—something to help them land gigs. The Drux twelve-tube amplifier is part of it too. Some guy named Vedder owns one.

"You know I don't interfere," Carol says. It's what she always says before she interferes. "But someday . . ." Her voice trails off. I can imagine her biting her lip. I've seen her do it a thousand times. "He's yours to deal with," she says finally, her point unspoken but made.

Sunlight glares off the windshield of a parked car, blinding me.

Bryan is mine. Mandy is too. Carol and I have an understanding. Before we married, she explained that she was at a point in her life where she could not sign up for mothering obligations. Nothing beyond the essentials. Self-nurturing would be her priority, she explained. It had to take precedence over what she called "other-nurturing." We discussed all this. I knew and respected her needs going in. I know and respect them now. My kids are less understanding.

I promise Carol I'll call when the car is fixed and I'm back on the road. She wishes me luck and reminds me about Sunday and the Kirtchner again. I send a kiss and hang up.

The folding door opens with a squawk, and I step out, escaping reflected glare, drawing in fresh air. My shirt is wet from armpit to waist and clinging to me.

Monk's Motorcycle Shop is a small cinder-block cube set on a narrow gravel lot a block off of Main Street. The inside smells of gasoline and stale cigarette smoke. An air conditioner rattles in the bottom half of the building's only window. The air it blows is mercifully cold.

Monk says I haven't changed in, what's it been, eight years? It's a welcome lie. His face has widened, his features coarsened. The years will do that. He still looks unruly, untamed, but definitely older too. He comes from behind his cluttered gunmetal desk. He still moves with a raw swagger. These days his long black hair is tied back and wild. With a rag, Monk wipes his hand and thrusts it toward me. Shaking hands with the guy is a quick wrestling match.

I explain about the car. He picks up the phone, dials someone, and lights a cigarette, waiting for them to answer.

"Head gasket," he says. "'72 Corvette. It's in front of Rita's."

"She a 427?" he asks me.

"454," I say. I hope Monk's impressed.

The cinder-block walls are covered with motorcycle posters. A dozen women or more—some pouty, some smiling, all tanned and scantily clad—straddle sleek riding machines. Most on red or blue bikes wear silky swatches and bubblegum smiles. Those astride black ones favor studded leather straps, short lengths of chain, and sultrier looks. They hold helmets because it's the law, like maybe they'd put it on to ride if someone asked them to go.

Monk hangs up. "You'll be ready to roll by three," he says. "Now what say we shoot some stick?"

"You're on," I say. "How about Randy and Murlene?"

"Okay," he says. His eyes seem less eager than his words. He makes two quick calls, though, and it's set.

We were children together, the four of us. I can't remember a time before Randy, Monk, and Murlene. We'd sometimes bloody one another's noses back then. Mostly we stood together, though, against the world's monsters, imagined and real. We shared pilfered cigarettes, drank creek water from the same tin cup, and pricked fingers to swear sacred oaths. One cool autumn night, dared and double-dared, we shed clothes and raced naked through the graveyard. Back then, friendship meant everything, and the truest truth in all the world was that we were friends.

Years passed and things changed. I yearned to be grown, to matter, to finally be done with endless childhood. By high school, we would brush past each other in hallways, hardly noticing. I got involved, as they say, running track, working on the yearbook. Mostly, I behaved myself.

Randy, born cute, grew into handsome. He dated older girls with smudged reputations and sailed through school with effortless Cs. He acted in school plays and, it was rumored, slept with a teacher or two.

Monk made the quickest exit from childhood. How I envied him that. School mornings, he earned good money changing oil at Kimbro's Garage. Afternoons he took vocational classes in the school basement, where he stood out among the potheads and drones. But Monk was neither of these. Before long, Kimbro had him doing tune-ups and overhauls.

Murlene stopped growing almost before she'd started. While her classmates grew taller and more awkward, she became quicker and more agile. One day she picked up a tennis racquet and served cannon shots to the girls on the high school tennis team. She soon was their leader and star. By her senior year she'd won the girls' state singles title. As Burkitt County's first state champion at anything, Murlene was paraded down Main Street, sitting in the back of a Cadillac convertible. She clutched roses and waved like a homecoming queen, which she clearly was not.

I'd first heard whispers the year before. Murlene always looked out of place in her lace tennis dress. Her hair, bright as a new copper penny, was cut short like a boy's, not at all like the other girls with their ponytails or shoulder-length flips. Murlene wore little make-up, and she never went on dates with boys. Not real dates. Some people whispered that it was unhealthy, how much time she spent with Miss Tanner, the new tennis coach. But everyone waved back to their bright champion as she rode down Main Street that sunny day, rode and waved in that convertible.

The night before graduation, the four of us met behind the football field against a graffiti-covered wall. It wasn't by plan. We'd hardly talked, in fact, for years. Murlene brought beer. Maybe she's the one who suggested it. In any case, we arrived that evening feeling free and filled with ourselves. We drank and laughed into the vast night sky. Boldly we told our dreams, told where we'd go, who we'd be, leaving this place behind. I've forgotten now what I said and what the others said. But I do remember how it felt lying there, gazing up at the star-filled, shimmery void. I felt whole and tiny and only a little afraid.

We all left town after graduation. The other three came back. Monk returned after his stint in the navy, followed by Randy the following year. Murlene was coaching tennis at a college out west when her father took ill. She returned to help with his nursery business shortly before he died. We gathered again at the funeral, the four of us. After the cemetery, we shot pool at Ham's Tavern, and within minutes, the years had fallen away.

Twice since we've gotten together—shortly after Wife Carol One died and then the evening before our twentieth class reunion. Each time, we'd play truth or dare with Murlene, as always, presiding as minister of truth.

Each Christmas we exchange quick notes. Birthdays too, when we remember. Murlene sees Randy often, she says, and Monk once in a while. For some reason, they don't get together though, only when I'm in town. In a letter, Murlene called me their catalyst. I've saved her letters and take them out to read sometimes.

Monk and I drop off my keys with Rita at the Huddle In. Now she recognizes me, says I should stop back later. I say I will but know I won't. Then Monk and I go down the block to Ham's Tavern.

Inside, my eyes slowly adjust to the room's dim lights. At one end of the bar, Ham chats to two customers. A third nurses his drink in a corner booth. In the back, Randy leans against the pool table lit by a low swag lamp. He's chalking his cue. He's posing, I know, but that's Randy.

"How the hell are you?" he calls, in his best radio voice. Randy's still tall and lean. His hair is shoulder length, highlighted and stylishly trimmed. Since I last saw him, he's added a mustache too.

"Compared to what?" I say. I choose a stick for myself. "Rack 'em up. Buck a ball all right with you?"

"Whatever you're ready to lose, Johnny boy."

"Ol' Monk wants some of that action too," Monk says. "Things been slow at the shop. I need to get well."

We lag off the far rail. Monk's ball taps the near rail, which means he buys first drinks. Randy short-arms his. Mine wins breaking rights easily.

As I spot the cue ball, Randy says, "You know Murlene will kick the crap out of you for starting before she's here."

"Let her try," I say, and I break with heavy overspin. A loud whack, and the balls fly everywhere. They careen off the bumpers and click on one another and slow to a roll and then stop. None fall though. Still, I feel this vibration inside, as if that rack of hard, colored balls has exploded inside me.

Randy tells me that he quit his radio job. "Manager was an SOB," he says. "On top of that, my afternoon callers turned mean. We're talking vitriol." He moves closer so only we will hear. "Besides, I already said what I had to say, said it ten times over or more."

"Our boy Randy photographs naked ladies now," Monk says.

"It's called boudoir photography. It's a small part of the business. Graduations, engagements, and family groups are most of it."

"You should see his newspaper ads. We're talking Victoria's Secret."

"Smart business," Randy says. He taps a finger on his forehead. "In a town this size, you've got so many graduates, so many engagements, so many anniversaries. You want more business, you better give them another reason for a photograph. Like a special picture for your husband's or boyfriend's eyes."

"And yours," Monk adds.

Randy acts as if he didn't hear, but I can see by his eyes that he did. "We shoot boudoir on Tuesdays. I spent over two grand on clothes. This wardrobe consultant comes in special. A makeup assistant too." Randy walks around the table for a shot.

"Tell him about the queers," Monk says.

Randy turns to face him now. "If homosexuals get pictures taken—which they don't—it's none of your goddamn business."

"That's not what Nita says. She says the local ladies aren't the only ones using your two-thousand-dollar wardrobe," Monk says, which confuses me, because last I knew, Nita was married to Randy—his third wife, I think.

Monk comes over next to me. "Sad to say our boy Randy's got wife problems again."

"Not anymore I don't," he says, "now that she's gone. Once I ditched her, my life got good."

Monk drains his beer before mine is half gone, and he orders a second round. "The way she tells it, she packed and walked."

"Well, hell. You don't believe everything a lying bitch says, now do you?" The last trace of humor is gone from Randy's smile. A stark grin is frozen there now. "Maybe you're screwing her too."

"Ol' Monk's got no use for your leavin's, son."

I step between them. "Boudoir photography," I say. "Sounds like creative marketing."

"Boy Scout to the rescue." Monk turns away, snorts a half laugh. "Whose shot is it anyway?"

For ten minutes we shoot pool and talk of the heat and baseball and classmates whose names I've mostly forgotten. Monk and Randy work their way back to joking with each other again as if their flare-up never happened. It was that way growing up. Fights were forgotten before the bloody noses dried.

I've got a run going, twelve balls, having just sunk a cross-table bank shot. I'm lining up a combination off the four ball when someone hits the end of my stick, which taps the cue ball and the eight beside it.

"Sonofabitch!" I wheel around.

It's Murlene. I grab her, lift her, and swing her once around. Her copper-colored hair has gray streaks now. Her green eyes still shine though, with her smile. A throaty laugh erupts from her. The smell of fresh-cut flowers is everywhere.

"You should have told me you were coming," she says.

"Didn't know until I got here. Passing through on business, tight schedule, and my damned car breaks down."

"Must be fate."

Murlene's words remind me of something Carol believes. People find ways to fulfill their unconscious desires, my wife contends, even if they have to sabotage themselves to do it. It's a useful belief, one that lets her explain away addicts and accidents and most of life's imponderables. It's useful too, because it keeps her world neat and understandable in familiar terms. When I get back to Chicago, I expect the Vette and me to be accused of unconscious intent. So be it.

"If it had to break down," I say, "what better place."

Murlene asks about Carol and the kids, and I say they're fine. I ask about Anne, Murlene's partner of nearly ten years.

"Anne's well," she says. "Thanks." Then she yells over for Ham to bring her a beer, and she reracks the balls. Randy was leading in the game she just disrupted. He doesn't object though.

"You still on the road," she asks, "selling?"

"They've got me cooped up in an office now. Every quarter the boss sends me out to check up on things." Said another way, I've been promoted. Vice president of marketing. But I don't say it that way. I know how it would sit.

"You still peddling blenders?" Randy asks. It's not an insult. That's how I said it last time here. Coming from him, though, it sounds like I'm selling door to door.

"M'Lady Kitchen Accessories. High-end small appliances—food processors, bread makers, juicers, dehydrators, all that. I'm in charge of national marketing."

Randy says, "Nita bought a bread machine. Two hundred

bucks. Bread sells for under a buck a loaf, and she buys this fancy machine and sacks of weird flour and what-all just so she can make her doughy bread."

"Hey, John," Murlene says, "tell your boss at M'Lady that you need a reliable company car."

I tell her that I'm driving the restored Corvette, that we're headed for a parting of the ways in Bowling Green tomorrow, a casualty of Mandy's tuition bills, the rush to get home, and Carol and the Kirtchner exhibition.

Murlene asks, "What's she paint?"

This will be difficult. But if anyone would understand, Murlene will. "She's not a painter," I say. "She works in mixed media. Collage."

Three blank faces.

Carol's planned press release says her works "combine diverse art forms to express her unique perspectives as a woman." That explanation, which sings in Chicago, would fall flat here.

"It's wall-hung art. What she does . . ." The third beer is getting to me. I struggle to put words to what she does, to construct a sensible way to explain it. I press the chill bottle against my forehead, draw in a deep breath, then plunge ahead.

"She writes these poems. Short ones. Philosophical," I say. "Three-line haiku. Feminist haiku. She writes them in miniature calligraphy—this really fine, ornate script—on scraps of ripped paper as small as postage stamps. She arranges them in collages with formed fabrics."

Worn bras starched stiff, yellowed girdles, and frayed garter belts—those are the fabrics Carol uses. She says it makes a statement, confronts the viewer, and forces her to reassess her frames of reference—whatever that means. Hell, I don't know. So, I skip the details about the fabrics. I've probably overexplained anyway.

"You have to see one to appreciate it." I'm groping for a way out. In truth, none of them would appreciate her art. Why didn't I realize that before I began? I blame the beer.

Randy is laughing. "People actually hang that crap in their homes?"

"Damn straight," I say. The truth is, Carol has only finished four pieces. They're huge and they take forever. None has actually sold yet. One hangs at a gallery off Rush Street, another at the Kirtchner. She's got the other two back at her studio. Reworking aspects, she says.

Randy parks his bottle on the radiator, grabs his stick, and stumbles toward the table. "Tell me, Johnny boy. What's the price tag on something like that?"

"All depends."

Murlene says, "Play pool, Randy. It's your shot."

"Just a little one. A five-by-seven, say," he says, coming closer.

"Art isn't sold by size," I tell him.

"I get twenty-two bucks for my best luster-tone five-by-seven. A boudoir photo will run you five bucks more," Randy says. He puts his bottle on the floor. "Those are my prices. Now you tell me, Johnny. What's crap-art go for in the city?"

"I'll guess, Randy," Monk says from across the table. "You want to hear my guess?"

"You got an answer for everything."

"I'll guess people pay as much," he says, "as you paid for all that fag lingerie."

"Man, you just can't get that off your mind, can you. Ol' Monk here is just dying to try on a feather boa? Is that it? Or maybe a thong?"

Murlene helps me keep them apart this time. She blocks Randy from going around the table, and I ask Monk what the hell time it is and didn't his guy promise to have the car back on the road by now? Monk has forgotten. He goes over to the bar to phone and give someone hell.

"Half an hour," Monk says when he returns. "Before three for sure."

I've lost track of the shooting rotation. I'm certain Randy's gone twice since my last turn, and Randy swears Monk shot both before and after him. Murlene suggests that we quit worrying about turns and score. Everyone agrees. No one had been keeping score in the first place.

Our game resumes, only now it's play without rules.

Murlene plops herself down cross-legged on the floor, posture erect like a tribal chief, the pool cue her warrior's spear.

"Truth or dare," she says, assuming her place as minister of truth, summoning us to our childhood game.

We're not up to taking dares anymore. "Truth," we answer as one.

"Truth," she intones. "Okay. Why'd you guys move back?

Monk sets his bottle on the table felt and looks at me. "Ten minutes out of boot camp, I figured it out—the motorbikes are no bigger, the girls no prettier, just because they're someplace else. So I live here, and I go when and where I want. Where you live don't count for shit. What matters is how."

"I'd have bet you'd be back," I say. "You had the job. You were dug in, not like the rest of us."

"Monk, I can understand. But I never thought I'd come back," Randy says. "Not in a million years."

"You had the looks," Monk says.

"And that voice," Murlene adds. "And a smile to open any door."

Randy lights a cigarette. "It was easy here," he says. "Everything was easy." He stares at the ember.

"Easy for you," Murlene says.

I line up a shot, realizing at the last moment that I'm shooting the nine, not the cue ball.

"There was this one day in LA," Randy says. "I'm wearing this fringed leather jacket and tooled cowhide boots, brand new duds, and I'm expecting traffic to stop or something. Then I see this guy with a jacket like mine, only his is beaded too, and his boots are snakeskin. He tells me he's been in town three months, and he says the only offers he gets have to do with his ass."

Monk lets out a yelp from his corner chair.

Murlene points her chalked spear at him. "Shut up."

"In Hollywood, they wanted plain-looking guys. Handsome is everywhere out there. They pave streets with it. So I tried Houston, tried Atlanta. I was in Birmingham interviewing for a graveyard slot on local radio, anything to get started. The station manager said it was mine, if I'd do this one small thing for him."

Even Monk is quiet now.

Randy takes a last draw on his cigarette and stubs it out. "Maybe I broke his nose. I didn't stay long enough to find out." He reaches for another cigarette and smiles at Monk. "At least here, it's women who crave my flesh."

Murlene gets to her feet and surveys the pool table. She can't find a shot, so she reracks the balls and breaks.

"And what about you, young lady," I say. "Why'd you come back to this quaint little town?" Implications hang in the air like Randy's smoke.

"I know the town and the town knows me." She's silent as she runs three balls.

"Come on, Mur," Monk says. "What the hell does that mean?"

"Means what it says."

"People talk," I say.

"You think I don't know?"

I shrug. "Chicago has all types of gays. Some flaunt it. Some live quiet lives, almost normal."

"Who are they?" she asks.

"What do you mean?" I ask. "They're gays. Lesbians."

"Okay, now tell me who I am."

"This is a trick question, right?"

"Answer, John," she says, pointing her cue stick at me. "Who am I?"

I shrug. "I'll play along. You are Murlene Tobin."

"And if I lived in Chicago, or someplace else, who would I be?" She pauses, then answers herself. "I'll tell you. I'd be another lesbian, that's who, someone for people to look at and categorize whether I'm one who flaunts it or maybe one who passes for normal."

"That's different. We knew you before, back when you were little Murlene."

"That's *always* been me. Don't you see? Before you knew—hell, before *I* knew—who I was." She sank to her seat on the floor. "You see me coming, you think, *Here comes Murlene.* Not *Here comes a lesbian.* This town knows me. They knew me first as Murlene. They talk. Of course they do. But they see the person too, because that's how they knew me first. Anywhere else, it was different. People never did see just me."

Randy says, "Don't try to tell me this town's special, that it's more tolerant. I've seen enough places to know better."

"Of me," she says. "They're tolerant of me. Because I grew up here. Anne would tell you a different story. Around here, she's the 'lezzy' living with Murlene and nothing more." She's on her feet again, her voice a sandy whisper. "You have no idea what she gave up for me."

Randy lines up a shot with the fat end of his cue. "It always seemed weird to me, two women like that. If you really think about it," he says, "and I'm not talking sex now, understand, but when you think about it, who knows better how to keep a woman happy? Another woman. Right?"

"A woman's happy or she's not," Monk says. "Men just get it into their heads that it's got something to do with them. That's just how women are. There's some who'll embrace their misery, cling like it's their lover. You think you can change a woman? You might as well try changing the weather."

"You've never been married, Monk," I say. "You don't know shit."

"Marriage is the worst kind of education a man can get, Johnny boy. It trains him to lie to himself," Monk says. "I ain't got to delude myself, just so's I can sleep at night. Ol' Monk, he looks the truth dead in the eye."

"And that truth is what?"

"Truth is this: A woman is mostly happy or she's not, and you can't change it, one way or the other. A fool goes crazy trying. That's when the woman's got him controlled."

"You're behind times," I tell him. "Ain't you heard back there in your cave? Women are liberated now. They don't need men."

"Like that new wife of yours? Open your eyes, son."

"We live our own lives, Carol and me."

"Tell me this, Johnny," Monk says. "You say you live your own lives, right? So why the rush to get back to Chicago?"

"The exhibit," I tell him. "I want it for Carol."

"Pussy-whipped." He says it as if I've proved a point. "Open your eyes, son. Your wife may spout modern lib bullshit about being free and independent. And you? You bust your ass trying to be—what did you call it?—her supportive male life partner? God, what a joke!"

"We're equals, Monk. That's how marriage works."

"Okay. Tell me this, and be honest. What do you think of her feminist art crap?"

"I don't know shit about art," I say. "What's it matter anyway? It's hers, not mine."

"And what's yours? Not the Corvette. You're selling that tomorrow to buy some fucking toy for a son who should be out on his own. Face facts, man. They got you jumping through hoops. It's time you figured it out."

"The trouble with you is you never grew up, Monk. You never made commitments, never took on obligations."

"You're the Boy Scout, not me. Women see someone like you coming a mile away. You're just what they want, what they need, a do-right man just aching to sacrifice."

"There's another word you don't understand," I tell Monk.

"I understand all right. When a woman needs someone to unload on, to dump on, she goes looking for one of you sacrificers."

The cue feels like a club in my hand. "When Carol got her chemo, I'd have gladly put the IV needle in this arm."

"That's different," he says. "I'm saying a woman will turn a man's best instincts against him. Think back before she got sick."

I can't though. I only remember the end. "Carol wasn't like that," I say.

"I won't talk bad of the dead," Monk says. He's pulling his punches now. "Do this. Some night when you're alone, when it's just you there—no music, nothing—think back. Be completely honest with Old John Fain. You owe yourself that. I bet you'll agree. Women are kudzu, man. They're kudzu."

Randy asks, "When did you get so cynical, Monk?"

"I just tell it like it is."

"The way you see it, Monk," Murlene says. "In life, people find what they look for. You get what you expect. Seek and ye shall find."

"Don't go biblical on me."

"I'm just saying, if you expect manipulation, by God that's what you'll find. Doesn't take a genius to see his favorite truths confirmed. Takes a half ounce of conviction and a well-slanted eye."

Monk laughs. "Look at our boy Randy here. What did he expect? Not a whole bunch, just one loving, caring wife. Is that what he found? No, ma'am. Poor Randy, he's oh-for-three and already back in the dugout, licking his wounds."

"Bitches," Randy mutters. "Every one."

"Sorry, Mur," Monk says. "Fortune-cookie philosophy just don't cut it in this world."

Murlene looks at her empty bottle. "You cynics got it easy. Don't believe nothing. Don't trust nobody."

"Hey," Monk says, "it keeps me sane."

"And alone," Murlene says.

"I find a warm body when nights are cold."

"Does it help, Monk?" she asks.

He shrugs. "It's what I need."

I've always looked up to Monk in a way. He's his own man. Ol' Monk, he does what he pleases and the world be damned. Now, as he leans against the pool table, bare arms folded across his chest, I'm not seeing our young rebel anymore. He's older, spreading, and turning sour. Maybe we all are. He still smiles though, cocksure as ever. But his eyes seem sad.

The mechanic shows up with my car and says it's ready to go.

The four of us settle up for drinks. I say my good-byes and swear an oath that I won't stay away so long next time. I mean it too. I will be back. I'll be back soon. And I'll stay longer then, maybe rent a room at the Holiday Inn Express over by the interstate and stay for a week or two. That much I owe myself.

Berliner

Sylvie, my wife, first told part of it as she cleared supper dishes almost three years ago. That was late 1960. "Aurie, dear," she said, "did you know that Jack Kennedy's a Gemini, the same as you?"

Sylvie had heard this from one of the few paying customers who patronized her new stitchery shop. As I understand it, some psychic had charted the heavens for the precise day Kennedy was born, and he determined that the man who would become our president in less than a month was destined for greatness. Of all his predictions, the one that seemed to impress her most was that during his second term, probably 1965, Jack Kennedy would barely avoid nuclear war. The details would remain hidden from the American people until early in the twenty-first century.

As we prepared for bed that evening, she told me the other part. I was stretched out on the floor, still breathing heavily from my nightly regimen of fifty sit-ups. Sylvie had tucked in Princess, her Pomeranian, for the night. Now, sitting at her vanity, she primped and fussed with her new corkscrew curls. "Jack Kennedy was born on May 29, 1917, too," she said.

"Amazing," I said. It was my birthday, but beyond that, it didn't seem to mean much.

"That makes you and Jack a perfect pair," she said. "You're identical Gemini." She never mentioned it again, at least not in front of me. But its importance took root. It grew and festered inside from that day forward.

I stopped watching television news, then started skipping entire newspaper sections. Still, try as I might, something about Jack would jump up and smack me.

Please understand. It is not that I am jealous of his photo-album family or youthful looks. I am not bad-looking myself. Nor do I envy him the applauding crowds. I sang "The Star Spangled Banner," after all, backed by the First Army Band before ten thousand people one Fourth of July in postwar Berlin. *Stars and Stripes* called me, Second Lieutenant Aurie Childress, the "Blond Sinatra." And it is not the way women melt around Jack Kennedy either. I've stayed faithful to Sylvie since the day we married, and there was only Eva before. But I will tell you quite honestly that there are still women in this town, quality women, who would meet me somewhere for a fun weekend if I'd just ask. Not that I think Kennedy would stray on his wife, or that he could, being president and never free to get away. I'm just saying that I have no reason to be jealous of the man.

No, what really rankled me—and I'm sure that she'd deny it, but I am just as sure that it is true—is that I somehow tarnished in Sylvie's eyes that day. Each morning over coffee and each evening before bed, I'd search her eyes for the old glint. But it had died.

So we drifted along, husband and wife out of habit.

Until this July, that is, when everything changed.

We sped south on Highway 25, returning to Spivey for the Rodell Fourth of July picnic. By tradition Sylvie's far-flung family gathered then. She seemed to bubble beside me, more effervescent than ever, anticipating the relatives ahead. Princess napped in her lap. A letter from Eva smoldered in my pocket, and my mind frantically tried to surround the pack of wild notions that the letter had set loose.

The Lexington radio station faded in and out. My Bonneville's crackling speakers rendered a Sinatra standard. Then Frank and Lexington gave way to a Knoxville station. Through a curtain of static came the strained voice of my identical Gemini.

As I reached by reflex to flick it off, Jack Kennedy proclaimed, "*Ich bin ein Berliner.*" My hand froze halfway to the dial.

Sylvie babbled on.

Had I gasped? I cleared my throat and swallowed. Princess's ears perked, then settled back. Ten thousand Germans cheered, and at that moment, I swear I could hear Eva's crystalline voice among them.

And so it was settled. The gods or the fates or whoever had sent a clear sign to me, and Jack Kennedy, of all people, was their messenger.

Eva Schmidt and I had shared one splendid week in Berlin in July 1948. I was her unbridled American and she my lusty *fräulein*.

Even now, I remember her adoring eyes, the strange way they smiled a second before her mouth did. I remember capturing fire-flies with her, learning to make glow-rings for our fingers. I remember Eva's walk, how her skirt and hair moved together. I remember laughter that didn't need a reason. I remember dark beers, warm pleasures, and mad passions that flowed to exhaustion.

Sylvie and I were already engaged by then and would marry that fall. But for seven short days, there was only Eva.

Before we parted that last day, waiting at the airdrome for the transport that would fly my unit out, I slipped the chain and dog tags off my neck and onto hers. She pressed a small gold charm, a sheep, into the palm of my hand. She tried to say something then, but the engine roar blew her words away, and it was time to go.

I was the last of my unit to board the plane. As we taxied to the runway, Lieutenant Spooner leaned close and said that he'd heard Eva Schmidt was the sixteen-year-old daughter of some dead Nazi colonel. Then he asked me in a most vulgar way what it was like be-ing with her. The question cost Spooner several good teeth. My answer nearly got me court-martialed. Fortunately, Captain Gross sided with the Blond Sinatra.

In the fifteen years since Berlin, memories of Eva sometimes drift-ed through my mind. At unexpected moments, I'd glimpse her reflection in beer. Summer evenings and flickering fireflies brought warm memories. In a crowd somewhere, I'd catch a hint of her cascading smile or the flowing wisp of her walk.

Her first letter was brief and tentative, awkward in its rusty English. It had arrived at our post office box in early June. She said that her friend at the American Consulate had traced me through the dog-tag numbers. She still lived in Berlin, she wrote, and her life had been mostly good. She had a ten-year-old son, Karl, but no husband now. She thought often of her American soldier. She hoped I was well, she wrote, and that life had been kind. I memorized Eva's address, tore the letter to shreds, and flushed it away.

I drafted a dozen replies. The one I eventually sent read much like hers. Simple, straightforward, skirting around certain things. I had no children. My singing career had fizzled. Through hard work and long hours, I'd built a small Pontiac dealership into southern Ohio's third largest. I'd recently taken up golf. Sylvie was not mentioned.

Eva's second letter arrived at the post office as we were packing for our trip to Spivey. I had loaded our suitcases into the Bonneville. Sylvie had packed sandwiches for us and special treats for Princess. On our way out of town, we stopped for paper plates and plastic forks. And one final stop, the post office.

I recognized Eva's lavender envelope and quickly folded it into my pocket. In my hands, I felt a photo bend.

We drove two hours before I stopped at a gas station outside Lexington. Behind the locked door of the piss-scented restroom, beneath a bare bulb, surrounded by graffiti and grease-covered tile, to the buzzing of a half dozen flies, I ripped open the envelope and read.

Her heart soars, Eva wrote, to learn that I remember her. She has known no one like her American lover. She has taken lovers since, several of them. There was a brief marriage. But no one satisfied her, brought joy, like her first—her unbridled American. Many nights she lies awake, remembering and wondering.

Her financial circumstance has deteriorated. She is forced to contemplate marriage to a widower who owns a large home, a sizable bank balance, and a hollow heart. But first she must know of her American. She would happily join him, even if in poverty, rather than enter into a convenience marriage. She humbly apologizes for such boldness, but she must know now if she lives still in his heart.

The tiny room felt suddenly hot. The stench of the restroom brought a sour taste into my mouth. My tongue felt like the sun-baked vinyl of a car dashboard. I turned on the water faucet, ran my cupped hands full, and drank. From the cracked mirror, a pale, bisected face with Picasso-set eyes stared out at me. I splashed water on my face and ran my wet hands over my hair. My heart raced. I steadied myself, hands grasping the rim of the sink, and looked with new eyes at the man in the mirror. His eyes were still blue and clear, his hair still blond and most of it there. His skin, older now, looked more weathered and wrinkled than I recalled. Character wrinkles, I told myself. If I'd changed, it wasn't that much. Surely she'd still recognize me.

A faint smile broke across the face in the mirror, a kind of dawning. Gradually it grew into a full, bright smile that became a laugh. I stuffed the letter back into its envelope and noticed the photograph, which I slid halfway out.

Eva had changed, yet she hadn't. The photo was a glossy black-and-white. Standing before the stone wall of a building that might be a castle, she squinted into bright sunlight. Her long shadow angled crazily across the stones. Eva looked slender now, less rounded than I remembered. She wore a plain, straight skirt and a white blouse that bore some sort of emblem. It might be a uniform, a governess, I thought, for no reason other than it seemed somehow right. Her smile, tight and thin, lacked the joy of our long-ago week in July, and her hair was cut short. Or it might still be long and pinned in back. There was no way to tell.

In the photo, Eva posed between two boys. Her right hand rested on the shoulder of a dark-haired boy with an imp's grin. To her left stood a taller, towheaded boy, unsmiling, his eyes downcast. Written in pencil on the back, the year 1963 and two names, Karl and Hans. I turned again to the photo. The blond boy was as tall as Eva. He looked much older than ten, probably a teen. The dark-haired imp, I decided, must be her Karl. But who was this other?

I turned away from the high, narrow window so light came over my shoulder and onto the photo. Could this boy Hans be mine? Surely she'd have said. More likely a nephew, I decided. Still, it seemed possible.

The doorknob turned. The door rattled against its latch, then came thuds, the pounding of a fist. "You okay in there, Mac? Lady out here says she's worried."

"Okay," I yelled, flushing the toilet, running water. "Be right out."

Life's decisions are rarely easy. Every choice has its pros and cons. So you can understand how, as we resumed our drive, so many pos-sibilities flooded into my mind. It was bewildering. And then, at that exact moment, Sinatra's song faded from the radio and the voice of Jack Kennedy, my identical Gemini, broke through the static and gave me an unequivocal sign.

"Berliner," he proclaimed, and thousands cheered.

With that word, my choice was made. It felt so right, the timing ideal. Sylvie would have family to lean on. I'd break it to her the next day. She had talked about moving back to Spivey one day. She want-ed to. It was my dealership that tied us to Ohio. She missed her fam-ily—she'd said that often lately. Now she'd be free to move back. Surely she'd see the positives in that.

Would she understand? Maybe not. It was hard to know. And where, I wondered, should I break it to her? The place out on Colton Road, I decided.

Her father deeded us two acres back when we married. The next spring, we poured a foundation slab. The dealership opportu-nity in Ohio opened up, though, before the concrete cured. We packed everything and went. The old place still meant something to Sylvie though. She hiked out there every time we came back to town.

We followed our lengthening shadows across the field. The earth around the slab was baked and cracked open. Sun-scorched weeds seeded Sylvie's skirt as we picked our way through. Thistledown tufts drifted on still evening air. Our slab lay well back from the road. The last time I'd driven by, it was hidden by weeds. But it wasn't hidden now. It was covered in graffiti of every imaginable sort—splashed paint and crude drawings, inked words of the vilest sort.

"Just look at that," I said.

"Leastways it gets used," Sylvie said. Her Kentucky accent had returned, as it always did coming home. "Better here than on bus station walls."

The woman would find the upside of a train wreck. Constant perkiness, so endearing in a young bride, gets to be downright annoying in a wife.

"Why they allow it," I told her, "I'll never understand."

She studied the slab like some museum exhibit. "They who?"

Feeling my irritation rise, I slipped a hand into my pocket to touch Eva's letter, to bolster myself. I drew a deep breath and dove in.

"I want a divorce." The words seemed to trip somewhere in the back of my throat and stumbled out.

Sylvie turned, her head and then her body, turned gracefully like a dancer. There was a placid expression on her face. How can she be so calm? Her eyebrows raised a bit then, arched up, asking me in their wordless way to repeat what I'd said. She hadn't heard.

I said it again.

She gasped. "What?" She'd heard that time.

"A divorce, Sylvie," I said much too loud.

She sat awkwardly. Involuntarily.

"We're different people now, different than when we married."

It sounded lame, and I knew it. On the drive here, I'd played things out in my mind, rehearsed them like a sales pitch. It had seemed so convincing, said in my head. But now, aloud, it fell flat.

"Of course we're different. Jeez, Aurie, we were kids." She got up, came toward me, her hand out. "That's no reason."

"It's not the same anymore, you and me." I backed up a step, two steps, without intending to.

"How?" she said. "Tell me how it's not the same?"

She'd made me feel twelve again, which seemed unforgivable of her.

"Talk to me, damn you!" In all the years we'd been married, it's the first time I'd heard Sylvie swear.

"I see it in your eyes," I said. "You used to care about things, what I said, what I thought. When things went wrong, you'd listen. Where'd that go?" That much was completely true. At least it felt true.

"For years I've listened to your complaints," she said, "listened to you gripe. It gets old, Aurie. Life's too short."

"You think I make it up? I don't. It's hard out there. Damn hard!"

She had her handkerchief out of her handbag, but there was nothing for her to use it on. "And I've got it easy?" Her voice was quiet now and hard to hear.

"Selling cross-stitch patterns and thread to your lady friends isn't the same," I told her. "Try having the district manager force a dozen loaded Bonnevilles on you when you can't even move the crappy Tempests on the lot."

"There're worse things in this world," she said.

"That's not my point." She was trying to soften me up, sprinkle her sunshine. Not this time, Sylvie, I told myself. Not this time.

Everything in her face got tight. "Exactly what is your point?"

I stared at the bunched skin between her eyes, kept looking there. "You don't care anymore," I told her. It all felt true in that moment. My reasons were reason enough. Eva was another matter altogether, not inconsequential, but irrelevant to us.

"Maybe," Sylvie said, "if you didn't always see gloom."

"I should be another you? Miss Pollyanna Ain't-it-wonderful?" I tried to say it respectfully, but I could see how she might not take it that way.

"You used to enjoy things," she said. "Remember? Somewhere along the way, you turned boring, turned into a grouch. Can't you just relax? Have fun?"

"That's what you think? You're stuck, married to a boring old fart?" I could feel things shift then, could feel myself take the offense again.

Sylvie dabbed at her eyes. "That's not what I said. You know it's not."

"Nobody's stuck here," I said. "Not you, and not me."

"I never said—"

"Give me a divorce, and go find Mr. Ignorant Bliss."

She squatted, picked up a handful of pebbles, and threw them at me, threw them point-blank at my face. I ducked. "You talk to me like I'm stupid," she yelled. "I'm not."

"Life's not all roses and spice, you know. There's more to it than tiny stitchery stuff, cute dogs, and star charts."

"Maybe it's nothing to you, but it's my business. My dog too, both *mine!*" She was close now, heat coming off her. "And what's that crack about star charts?"

"You're always gushing that stuff, about fates in the stars and destinies."

"When?" she said. "I don't believe that stuff."

There had been several times. Quite a few. Trouble was, the only ones that came to mind were from years ago. "Kennedy and me." I tried to keep any hint of triumph out of my voice. "You remember?"

If she'd snapped "no," I'd have taken it for a lie. But Sylvie, for all her faults, is no actress. Her blank stare was real.

"Identical Gemini?" I reminded her. "Remember?" I could see she didn't though. "Someone told you about this magazine article. It was right after Kennedy's election. You remember . . . about his star chart?"

"The nuclear war prediction?"

"That's the one!"

"And you think I believed that? It's there to sell magazines, Aurie."

"But there was more," I told her. "You remember. About Jack Kennedy and me being born the same day? How we're identical Gemini?"

There was a look of exasperation on her face. "I don't remember. Jeez, Aurie, it was a stupid horoscope!"

I could feel things slipping away. "You haven't looked at me the same since."

"And how have you looked at me? Like I'm nothing, like I don't matter. I'm supposed to listen to your crap, just agree when you say the world's a sewer?" She wasn't sprinkling sunshine anymore.

"A little sympathy's all I ask," I said.

"Sorry, Aurie. The world isn't a sewer. Everyone's not lining up to dump on you."

"You used to care," I said. "What happened?"

"We were young, fresh out of high school," she said. "I thought you were some sort of god."

"Not even close," I said. "I'm a man who wants a woman to love him." The memory of Eva's smile flashed across my mind in that moment, her marvelously spreading smile, the one that starts in her eyes.

"I did. I do," she said. "But with you, nothing comes back."

"Who put a roof, a damn fine roof, over your head and always food on the table. And cars."

"Not love though," she said, her voice gone hoarse. "Did you *ever* love me?"

"Don't be ridiculous," I told her.

"When, Aurie? Tell me when."

"In the beginning. For years."

She turned away. Her gaze went to the slab, to the scrawls there. "Maybe you did."

She looked tired now, as tired as I felt. You don't get to be the number three dealership in southern Ohio, though, by letting fatigue matter. The moment seemed right. "Let's end the marriage," I said. "End it now."

In silence Sylvie twisted her handkerchief for the longest time. She sighed. "I've wasted too many years on you," she said at last.

Just that fast, I was free. There would be formalities, of course, legalities and explanations to concoct, but I knew it was ended then. Standing there, I could hardly believe it.

Would Eva like America? Would she need a green card, a passport or visa or something like that? There was so much to check in to, so much new to learn. In the morning, I decided, I'd write to her. Better yet, I'd write tonight.

Sylvie looked out across the field standing tall with blue blooms of lanky-stemmed chicory. My gaze followed. The red sun was low, almost down, our shadows long. From the flowers, one tiny yellow beacon rose up, blinking, and then another.

"Fireflies," she said softly.

I saw them then, hundreds dotting the field, rising and blinking their secret code.

"Remember that evening?" she said. "The summer before we married? It was right here. Like children, we chased fireflies."

I looked at her, confused, searching my memory.

"I taught you," she said, "to make glow-rings."

Now I couldn't answer, couldn't stop the carnival in my brain.

"Don't tell me," Sylvie said, a hint of scolding in her voice, "that you've forgotten that."

9 780813 125404